I0671110

Not Lost—

Just Not Found

Not Lost—
Just Not Found

A Novel by
Daniel Hill Zafren

TIME TREASURES
BOOKS

Copyright © 2008 by Daniel Hill Zafren

Published by Time Treasures Books, West Jefferson, North Carolina

ISBN: 978-0-9778892-6-6

Printed in the United States of America

Cover design by Susan Newman Design Inc.

Not all who wander are lost

J.R.R. Tolkien.

ONE

I have no idea who I am.
I don't know what I want to do with my life.
Why am I so ordinary?
How can I overcome feeling like a simpleton?
How do I tell the difference between what is real and what I think is real?
What is happiness, and will I ever be happy?

He would be a wealthy man if only he had a dollar for each time he heard such dejected statements and searching questions. If you do not know where you are to begin with, a categorization or label of being lost does not seem appropriate. A more apt description might be that the individual has yet to be found. Whatever it is or might be, such is debilitating, confusing, and depressing. Especially is this the case for young people.

Parker Benson deals with the not yet found young people. The early travelers on the road of life are straddled with so many pressures, true and imaginary. Knowing that illumination and comfort come with time and experience does not translate easily into advice that gives much solace. It is nearly worthless to indicate that so many others share the same kind of disconnection from society. Others do sense that their individualism, whatever that might be, is beyond attainment. To gain a firm footing on trembling ground is no easy task. To feel whole when parts are undefined and untested often appears beyond reach. No wonder a whole generation is disenchanted.

What made it more real, more compelling, was that at one point in his life he was that way too. Roll back some fifteen years when he first started college, he had not the foggiest notion what he wanted to do with his life. Being able to talk about a place he had also been lent credibility to his observations and bolstered his credentials to offer advice as a licensed psychologist. Wrestling with that same oppressive feeling built enduring empathy. It prompted an understanding and compassion for these mental and emotional struggles. His education and training allowed him to clinically describe the anguish, the frustration, and the despair. However, reality and theory are distinctly different unless and until they become one.

As man is miniscule as he gazes out on the universe, Parker considered himself a tiny force as he looked out over the broad expanse of the campus of Blantyre University. The University is a picturesque New England liberal arts college with a mushrooming enrollment to match the increasing national attention and awards given to the curriculum and teaching staff. Commencing his third year as the University Psychologist, his role varied with the troubles and conceptions students brought to his office. In most instances, success came not with him helping the students but rather in guiding them to help themselves. Self-enlightenment and self-discovery are major and lasting accomplishments. Gaining insight leads to the means of viewing the outside world with confidence and vibrato.

Over the prior two years there had been little time to devote to himself. Establishing his posture at the University and acquainting himself with all of the accountability standards were quite time consuming. Detailed reports were required for all of his actions. The death of his parents just eight months apart burdened his time even more. The frequent trips to Florida to be with them during terminal illnesses and their final days consumed large doses of his energy. Fortunately, Clarissa, his sister, lived in Florida near the retirement home and was able to monitor and care for them daily. His visits, while frequent, were more supportive for Clarissa than for the folks who were often unable to recognize him. The family had always been close and loving, and that contributed so much to peace-of-mind. Clarissa had not been so fortunate. The loving home could not fully cushion two bad marriages. At least there had been no children involved, and she had finally found a rewarding occupation as a real estate agent.

For Parker, meaningful romantic relationships had been scarce. Just because his sister had been burdened with bad unions did not scare him away from an involvement. He was not sure what kind of woman could fulfill his yearning for companionship and raising children. Yet, he was confident that she was out there and a connection just waiting to happen. He only had to find her just as he had discovered himself. It was not accurate to describe it as an act of locating her. It was more as recognizing her qualities when their paths might cross.

The walk from his office to the faculty housing on a hill just beyond the campus was always invigorating. The school grounds were beautiful and well maintained. The air seemed to carry special messages to his senses. Each season had its smells, its distinct tribute to days passed and as a preview of times to come. The air cleared cobwebs from his mind, and deep breaths fortified his body. It was a special transition time either for going to work or returning home.

The year-round faculty housing consisted of terraced town homes, the higher the units the more commanding were the views of the valley and the mountains beyond. Avoiding using his car when he could walk, he had to climb the steep steps to get to his unit near the top terrace. Even that exercise was beneficial, and once inside the cozy confines of his unit he was prepared for his cup of hot chocolate and to settle in the easy chair looking out on the countryside and to read. He congratulated himself on finally mastering the art of relaxation.

There was an hour for him to lounge in the chair and sip the silky liquid before he had to start out to the Dean's dinner for new faculty members. Even an hour would ordinarily be enough time for him to catch a glimpse of his past or to read a passage from a favorite book. He was at this moment just content to let the soothing quiet permeate his being. People erroneously think that the past, the present, and the future are separate and independent. Actually, they are intertwined. They are building blocks erecting the composite of who the person was, is, and will be. Not really three distinct persons but basically one and the same. This is such a difficult concept for young people to grasp.

The Dean's dinner was held in Keystone Hall, the administration building. Housing a large impressive hall, the walls are lined with paintings and sculptures. A catered affair with tables of eight set up and a large table with appetizers and wine bar set off to the side. Some of the faces he did not recognize, and he presumed these were the newest faculty members. With big fanfare, they would be introduced just before the serving of the dessert.

Parker noticed a rather interesting looking woman sipping wine as she stood off to one side. He guessed her to be in her thirties. Her form-fitting blue dress revealed a slim frame, so she evidently took good care of herself. Straight brown hair fell to the shoulders, and as he approached her he saw the eye color matched her hair. A hint of a smile on thin lips emerged as she saw him draw near.

He mustered up his warmest smile. "A food or idea merchant?"

A pleasant voice matched the demure appearance. "Are those my only two options?"

"Certainly the obvious ones."

"Not everything is as it may appear."

"How well I know that." He extended his hand to meet hers. "Parker Benson."

She grasped his hand warmly. "A food or idea merchant?"

"Must be an echo in here. Neither one. Not everything is as it may appear."

"Yes. There is definitely an echo in here. I suppose I should only say those things that may bear repeating. I am Myrna Ocelot. I am Dean Shapiro's new administrative assistant, a fancy term for his secretary."

"I am the school shrink. The students refer to me as the school skunk. Most of them find my advice stinks."

"Then you better steer clear of echoes."

"See, you give better advice than I do."

Her broad smile revealed straight teeth, and her glasses could not hide a twinkle in her eye. "A lucky statement, no doubt."

"Actually, it is because I often tell them what they don't want to hear. They also come to me for answers, which I really can't give them. I try to guide the questions inward so that they find their own answers. What they find most difficult to comprehend or accept is that not all questions have answers. Sorry to be so serious."

"Please don't apologize. It is a serious time for these youngsters. I was an administrative assistant to the academic dean of the University of Virginia system before coming here, and the emotional grappling is widespread."

"That it is." A moment's pause for him to record in his own mind how pleasant it was to talk with her. The motions and voices surrounding them blurred into the background. He continued attempting to fully capture and retain the moment, "I don't know about you, but I went through it myself."

She smiled again, moving slightly closer and speaking in a more hushed tone, "I did too, at least a couple of times that I know about."

"Once is enough."

Just then they were interrupted by an announcement that the attendees be seated for dinner. Myrna was seated with Dean Shapiro at the chancellor's table, Parker was placed far back in the hall with other non-faculty members of the University staff. He knew them well as they were often grouped together. There was some lively dinner conversation that made the dried chicken palatable. The speeches and introductions were also mercifully brief, and the gathering broke up right after Dean Shapiro thanked the crowd for attending and wished all a successful academic year.

Myrna came over to say good-bye. "The Dean is driving me home, but I did want to tell you how much I enjoyed our chat, no matter how short it was." She extended her hand and he grasped it firmly, noticing that there was no ring on her left hand. "You are easy to talk with. That's a refreshing experience. I am sure you are very good in your profession."

Reluctantly, he let go of her hand. "It was my pleasure. You made my evening memorable."

He watched as she left, his eyes riveted to her shapely calves below the hem of her blue dress. That image stayed with him well into the night. These are the sort of snapshots for the mind to dwell upon.

*I've learned that people will forget what you
said, people will forget what you did, but
people will never forget how you made them feel.*
Maya Angelou

TWO

Two weeks into the new semester and Parker's daily appointment calendar was nearly full each day. The political and economic climate of the country was particularly volatile, and those kinds of conditions could only exacerbate any of the pressures found in or related to academic studies. Freshmen were an especially vulnerable group. For many of them it was the first extended time away from home. The demands and expectancies of a large college are often a far cry from a smaller and more familiar high school environment. The transition can be a rude and daunting experience.

That Monday late in September was cloudy and a cold wind blew across the valley. At times the mountains blocked the winds. On this day the mountains funneled the winds downward and accelerated their downdraft to the lands below. He was not a believer in omens but the chill made him put up the collar of the raincoat so it was snug against the back of his neck. As he trudged toward his office he tried to think of some concocted scheme to go to Dean Shapiro's office so that he could see Myrna. The wind seemed to blow away any of the ideas he could come up with. As always, the direct approach might be the most effective one.

Richard Clemmons was his nine o'clock appointment. Awaiting his arrival, Parker studied the young man's file. That file contained the student's personal information as well as the pre-visit questionnaire the student had to fill out when making the appointment. The item Parker generally checked first was the student's own description of why the campus psychologist

11

was being consulted. The cryptic description by this student captured his interest – *summer trauma.*

The young man was a senior, and that was another aspect that intrigued Parker. He had not seen him before, his grades were good, and he was on the track team. Being well balanced in school usually reflected a placid home life. Exceptions could easily arise, and a person's rather settled life could be jolted to an extreme at any moment. The volatility of life itself is often reflected in its component human parts.

There was one receptionist to greet appointees for Parker as well as the other non-faculty administrative personnel. All of these offices were in a small building on a far edge of the campus, actually a hefty hike from all of the academic buildings. The building at one time housed care-taking equipment but had been renovated to offices when the growth of the university spurted. When the telephone rang, he knew it was Arlene Peters announcing that his appointment had arrived.

Parker went out to greet the young man. Richard was tall, muscular and deeply tanned. He wore a suit and tie, and Parker interpreted that as a sign of respect. Of course, he had given up ties himself except for formal occasions, and he generally wore a sports jacket with an open shirt or a turtleneck sweater. He led Richard into the office, closed the door and beckoned him to sit in the chair in front of the desk. Parker sat behind the desk and noticed Richard glancing around the room. "Looking for the couch?"

"Yes," Richard offered in a strained voice.

"I don't use the couch technique. I like the people that I see to feel that I am their equal rather than someone looking down on them. I much rather develop a relationship as friends rather than one as doctor-patient. So, try to think of me just as a professional friend."

Richard smiled slightly and Parker sensed that he had succeeded in putting the young man somewhat at ease. To continue in that vein, he asked him a number of general questions about his studies, which professors he found most interesting, and the recent movies he had seen and enjoyed.

After chatting for some moments, Parker then asked forthrightly, "Well, Richard, why do you feel you need a professional friend?"

Richard diverted his eyes out the window. Maybe he was looking for a transformed inner will to utter the words describing the trauma he had experienced. It took a tense moment for the young man to compose himself. Not looking directly at Parker, his gaze shifted from the bookshelves to the floor. He began his story in a weak voice at odds with the visual strength of his body. "My family lives near the beach in Long Beach on Long Island. I got a job for the summer as a lifeguard at the beach. That is why I have this tan. Actually, it is a pretty boring job which does not pay very well. I suppose the only reason I took it was because of all of the girls that hang around the lifeguard stations. One girl especially attracted me not because she was beautiful but because she was so bubbly all of the time. Her high excitement with everything was contagious. I was drawn to her. We started dating. She lived with her mother in a house in a poorer section of the town, although that made no difference to me. Her mother was strange. Each time I would come to the house, she never smiled and hardly said two words. There was a glassy look in her eyes. I didn't want to press it with Laura, and figured she would tell me about her mother when she wanted to. I sort of figured that Laura's bright outlook was an effort to compensate for her mother's dreariness. I respected her for that, but that was not enough after awhile. By the time our fourth date rolled around, her mother's weirdness was starting to freak me out and Laura's enthusiasm could not overcome the repulsion I felt towards her mother, so I decided to stop seeing Laura. I was going to tell her when we got back to her house."

There he stopped for a minute as if he was reliving that evening. When he continued his voice weakened further. Parker had to strain to hear. "Laura invited me in the house, and I was going to tell her as soon as we sat in the living room. First, she went to check on her mother. There was a terrifying scream. I rushed upstairs. Laura was leaning against the frame of the bathroom door sobbing and shaking violently. I looked past her. Her mother was lying slumped over on the floor in a pool of blood. She had slashed her wrists." Another pause and Parker noted tears at the corners of Richard's eyes. "Laura took it very, very hard. Natural, I suppose. She blamed herself for her mother's death. She has since clung to me for comfort and support. I was trapped. I am still trapped."

It was quite a story and a troubling situation. Parker needed some more information before he could make any attempt at prompting a healing process. "Have you talked this over with anyone, particularly your parents?"

"Yeah, I talked with my parents numerous times. They do not think I owe anything to this girl. They say I should just walk away."

"Probably sound advice from a parental point-of-view."

"I guess so. I just can't do it. She is like a wounded animal. I just can't leave her to die."

"So what do you feel you should do?"

"Believe me, I am tormented by this. I just don't know what to do. That's why I have come to see you. I hope you can tell me the right thing to do."

Parker studied the young face. The anguish was concealed by bright, youthful eyes. It was evident in his voice, however.

Parker spoke calmly and deliberately. "It is not for me to decide what is right for you, or even what might be best for her. The only thing I can do is to talk this out with you so that you can reach some resolution on your own. A composite of emotions are playing havoc with your life. You need to sort them out so that you can regain composure and carry on. Your studies and your athletic involvement should not be neglected. Laura needs to grope with her own demons to get on with her life. It might be a good idea if she saw a professional. She would benefit from talking this out."

"When the police came to investigate the death, they suggested that to her."

"What was her reaction?"

"She said she needed me more than anything else."

"Undoubtedly you feel great sympathy for her plight, and it is admirable that you are willing to share her pain and want to be there for her to lean on. You also feel guilty because you were going to break up with her and that would be a double blow to her. As I see it, and believe me you are not in an easy situation capable of a quick solution, you have translated all that you think and feel into an obligation towards Laura. Has it ripened into an irrevocable commitment? Do you want that?"

"I am not sure I understand."

"Are you ready to marry her?"

"Of course not."

"Do you want to drop out of school and live with her?"

"No."

"Do you want to undo the hurt the tragedy has heaped on her?"

"Yes."

"Can you realistically do that?"

"I can be there for her."

"There for her what?"

"To be her friend."

"Yes, you can be that if you set the boundary for it."

"I think she expects more from me than that."

"Are you ready to meet her expectations even if those clash with the expectations you have of yourself?"

Richard jumped to his feet and went to the window. He stared out to a world that maybe he was not ready for. "You make it all sound so complicated."

"If it was simple, you would not be in my office. If all occurrences and their meanings and interpretations were straightforward and if all relationships were untroubled, I would not have a job."

"I can't just do nothing."

"That is not a viable option. It may not even be proper to think of this as the right or best thing to do. Perhaps, you need to look deep inside yourself and decide overall what is the most honest thing you can do."

"A hard road for one like me who suddenly realizes that I do not know it all as I thought I did. You mention my expectations. I am not sure I have ever had any of them. What are my expectations, anyway? It is more of what my parents and society want of me than what I want of myself."

"Do you have your own dreams?"

"If I do, I don't understand their place in the scheme of things."

"Don't be afraid to dream, to hope. There is a future in the cards totally your own. Perhaps that is a place for you to start sorting all of this out."

"I suppose I am basically immature and inexperienced."

"Just the fact that you are wrestling with such a serious happening shows great maturity. If you have confidence in yourself, you will have foresight."

Richard turned and gave Parker a half of a smile. "You should put a sign outside reading that there are no answers in here."

"Did someone steal it again?"

Richard laughed, probably his first laugh in a long time.

At the end of the day, after counseling a number of momentary human failings, Parker's mind returned to Richard's dilemma. He hoped that the young man would come talk to him again as he had encouraged him to do. He had the feeling that he would make up his own mind and stick to it. He was not sure what he would do if he were in his place. Compassion is a truly two-edged sword. Compassion is a trait missing in much of the animal world, and it can be either a dire human weakness or a great human strength.

To accomplish great things, we must not only
act, but also dream; not only plan, but also believe.
Anatole France

THREE

The large clock above the doorway reminded her of the passing of time. In this instance it was excruciatingly slow. It had been two weeks since the dinner. Myrna Ocelot thought, or at least hoped, that Parker would have come to Dean Shapiro's office to see her long before this. Maybe she had read the signs wrong. After all, she was out of the man-woman relationship development for many years. Even with the brief exchange, she sensed he had an interest in her. In a subtle manner she had tried to convey that any interest was mutual. In a small way it was exhilarating to experience such a feeling. It had been far too long. Having an eleven-year-old daughter was truly a mixed blessing. She loved Gabby greatly, and the child was animated, warm and loving. The youngster filled the house, wherever that might be, with activity and laughter. Yet, it detracted from her journey for adult pleasure and companionship. It was more than seven years since the divorce had been finalized, and she could count on one hand the dates she went on since then. Even if he initially found her interesting, as soon as a man discovered she had a child, further involvement was curtailed. Myrna was optimistic that the move to Blantyre would prompt a new beginning for her. Meeting Parker had keenly encouraged her.

Myrna's life had been a roller coaster ride. The heights and depths often left her unsettled and frazzled. Her resolve remained firmly intact. The marriage had been unfortunate. She had been too young, too inexperienced to recognize an underlying incompatibility. Gabby's birth was the devastating blow to the already shaky marriage. Finding the job at the University of Virginia had been a challenge and a test of her determination. Being a single mother, working full time, and trying to recover from emotional disappointment and frustration might wear many women down. She, however, was not going to let any aspect of her life discourage her from making the best of each moment for the two of them. The inner strength was a sustaining and further motivating factor that gave her the incentive to move to a fresh locale and seek a new job. It gave her the impetus to plot getting to know a man she had only seen and talked to briefly.

It turned out she did not have to put any plan into execution. Dean Shapiro asked her to call Parker Benson and schedule an appointment for him to come in to discuss some of his reports.

That turn of events also worked out well for Parker. He had been hesitant, as a possible remnant of the bashfulness he experienced as a youngster, to go in on his own. It might not bode well to display an easily deciphered overt interest in Myrna. The appointment was set that he come over after his last appointment that day, which would be at four o'clock.

When Parker arrived at Dean Shapiro's office, Myrna was filing some papers in one of the cabinets in the outer office where she had her desk. Dressed in a white blouse and a black skirt, she looked fresh as if it was the first thing in the morning rather than late in the day. As she turned towards him, the alluring feminine form was not lost on him.

He spoke first, his voice lowered to match the quietness of the room. "Hello, young lady."

She smiled, "Forgot my name, didn't you?"

"No, Myrna, I did not. I just wanted to emphasize how refreshingly young you look."

"Flattery will get you almost anywhere."

"Would it get me a date with you?"

"You doctor types sure don't waste any time or words."

"Not when we are fixed on what we want."

It was time for her to seal her fate. "I have an eleven-year-old daughter."

He hesitated for a few seconds. "Is there a husband in the picture?"

"No. I have been divorced for a long time."

"Phew. I thought I would have to make a hasty retreat. I have no wife, no children, no mind to change. Now you know all about me and I know all about you. A date seems in order to me."

Somehow she knew he would not disappoint her. "Then, I suppose I must accept."

It was set for Saturday night. He would take her to one of his favorite restaurants, *Mountain View*, which uses local produce whenever it can in preparation of special French cuisine. Parker offered that Myrna could bring her daughter along but she wanted to be alone with him. Gabby was responsible enough so she would not need a babysitter. In fact, she would be excited that her mother was going out on a date. Gabby was the one who often encouraged her to accept if an invitation came along.

Being excited turned out to be too tame a word. Gabby took sheer delight in teasing her mother about the forthcoming event. In fact, she composed a little poem that she chanted repeatedly.

> *Dr. Benson is coming calling,*
> *In love my mommy is falling,*
> *Mommy can't wait,*
> *Mommy is going on a date.*

Saturday evening arrived, and Parker stood on the porch

of the small Victorian house Myrna was renting and hesitated a moment before he rang the bell. He could not shake the feeling that a new chapter in his life's story was about to begin. How often had he urged others to take hold of opportunities when presented to them? Now was the chance for him to live by his own words.

A young smiling girl opened the door. She was almost a miniature replica of Myrna, right down to the same straight brown hair and sparkling brown eyes, even including the glasses.

"Welcome, Dr. Benson, she said in a high pitched voice. "I am Gabby."

"Well, I did not expect to be greeted so warmly. I guess your mother told you all about me."

"You'll have to come in to get warm. That part I can figure out for myself."

He entered the hallway and followed Gabby into the small sitting room. "Mom is almost ready. She'll be down in a minute. She asked me to keep you busy. Sit down, if you want to."

"Thanks, Gabby. I think I will rest my tired bones for a moment."

"How do you know when a bone is tired?"

"It has a sort of aching feeling."

"One bone, or all of them?"

"It really is a matter of emphasizing that the entire body aches from weariness."

"Mom said you were smart."

"She did, did she? I don't know about that. I just know that I try to figure out how I feel, and my job is to figure that out for others."

"Yes. She told me you are a psychologist. Did I get that right? I practiced saying it."

"Perfect. Have you started school yet?"

"Oh, yes. It is only two blocks away so I do not have to ride the bus. I like that. I get to sleep an extra fifteen minutes."

"Made any friends yet?"

"Not any close ones like I had back home, I mean back in Virginia. There are a number of cliques, and mom has always said I should try to avoid them because it limits knowing other girls."

"That sounds like good advice."

"I have a really wise mother. You should get to know her better."

"I plan on doing just that."

"She also listens to me."

"How so?"

"She asked me if she should go out with you."

"And what did you tell her?"

"I told her she should have a good time. After all, she is not getting any younger. I don't want her to be alone when I leave home."

Parker laughed. "Do you plan on leaving soon?"

"No, don't be silly. But if I don't go to Blantyre I will go away to college."

"What do you want to study?"

"I am too young to know that yet. Mom says not to rush myself into making any adult decisions while I am still a kid."

"Some more good advice."

Myrna entered the room. She was wearing a tailored pants suit, and there was a youthful flare about her. Her voice was playful. "I heard some lively conversation down here. Sounded like Gabby was talking your ear off."

Parker interjected, "Let's not start on that. I had enough trouble explaining about tired bones. I do not think I could adequately explain how talk can remove an ear. However, I was just about to ask her for permission to take you out."

Gabby giggled robustly. "Sure it is. Just have her back real early."

Last minute instructions by Myrna, emphasizing that Gabby could call on the cell phone if there was any problem. A warm hug and they left, not without Parker winking at Gabby.

The restaurant was perched at the outskirts of the town, with large picture windows allowing the patrons to see the mountains as they tested the creations of the chef. Even at night, as now, when they walked from the parking area the mountains loomed as huge black images against a star-studded sky. The night chill, a prelude to another cold New England winter, left the air clear and crisp. She held his arm, and it felt good for Parker to have someone at his side. For her, it was comforting to hold tight to a person, symbolizing a need we all have.

The dinner was excellent, a real culinary feast. Both ordered a salmon Caesar salad. A toast of wine, and the varied conversation flowed with ease. They were not rushed to finish and leave, and even the night seemed especially hospitable to two wandering souls at a resting place in their sojourn.

"You never married?" Myrna asked with a tinge of selfish curiosity.

"No. I have yet to find a rapport with any woman." He fell silent for a moment. "But, I haven't given up. Have you sworn off another marriage?"

"No," she responded with half a smile. "I not only want to find a man I am comfortable with but he has to accept a ready-made family. I'm at the end of my child-bearing days, and the corpus of men who might accept a package of me and Gabby is, as far as I can tell, nearly non-existent."

"Does that sadden you?"

"No, not really. I just need to face a strange sort of reality and accept it. I would like someone for me, although Gabby fills my life."

"Do you mind that we speak on such a personal level?"

"Not if it as friends. I would not like the psychologist in you to be the one I am speaking to."

He smiled and reached across the small table for her hand, pleased to find it soft and warm. "That part of me is left at the office."

She smiled broadly. "You get an A for a correct response, kind sir."

"It is not always easy to do, but I find that my life needs to be separate and apart from my professional being. Each can intrude on the other but I keep it minimal."

"That's good because I am a firm believer in the separation between business and personal lives. A man would also have to be comfortable with me. While I do try to stay in shape, I have a case of the FS."

"That isn't a psychological term."

"Certainly not. It means various parts of my body are flabby and saggy."

Parker laughed. Myrna was a candid and humorous woman. He liked those traits. "Interestingly, I have a case of the D."

"That sounds serious."

"It sure is. It is decay in the replay."

"Although we have a way to go yet, I really don't mind growing old. It is just that everything in our existence glorifies youth and treats aging with disdain."

"It is a matter of practicality. The economy and much more are driven by and geared to the youth culture. The youth culture thinks, or rather is led to believe, that it should be as the economic interests string them along. The big irony is that the youth culture does not understand itself and does not know how to use the power it holds within its grasp."

"I fear for Gabby growing up in this troubled world."

Pressing lightly on her hand, he spoke softly, the words being spoken as if by their own accord. "She is fortunate to have a mother in touch with reality who will guide her through the trying instances."

"I think that is the nicest thing anybody has ever said to me." She placed her other hand over his. Her heart had already broken away from its confines.

Parker was not sure what he felt. He was so at ease with this woman and captured by her essence. She was not attractive by Hollywood standards, and the glasses even made her appear matronly. Yet, a soft spoken and gentle mannerism, coupled with an attentive and sharp mind, comprised an alluring and heart-warming package. He even felt a strong sexual attraction to her, and that was especially significant because of its rarity.

She invited him in for some hot chocolate, and Parker felt this was another connection since it was also his favorite beverage. Gabby was asleep on the sofa, the television still on. Myrna carried her upstairs and returned in a few minutes. "She didn't even wake up."

"All of her questions will have to wait until the morning."

"There will be a barrage of those, I am sure. Come into the kitchen while I heat up the milk."

They talked at length over the savory brown liquid. Parker told her about his deceased parents and his sister in Florida. Myrna's parents were also deceased, and she wished that Gabby could have had close grandparents. Such can be a rich experience. Her brother and sister still lived in the Virginia town where she was born and raised. Both had children and rocky marriages. Such is a symptom of the modern age where technology seems to make relationships narrowly programmed rather than expansively natural.

They kissed at the front door before he left. The kiss spoke their thoughts. Each was reluctant to admit and yet secretly wished that this was the beginning of a special relationship. A night can hold many dreams.

> *There is no end. There is no beginning.*
> *There is only the passion of life.*
> Federico Fellini

FOUR

On Monday morning the walk to the office was particularly invigorating. Despite the chilly autumn day, Parker had a warm sensation throughout his body. Just when he was beginning to doubt that a special woman might enter his life, Myrna represented both a promise and a challenge. He knew better than to jump to conclusions, but since he felt so comfortable with her he eagerly awaited their next get together.

His schedule was full, including another senior, a student he had not seen before. Sheila Levine was an active and high achiever on campus. The reason she put on the pre-visit questionnaire for needing to see him was the one intriguing word *duress*. Cryptic answers often reminded him of the classic college story of the erratic Philosophy professor and his class on Existentialism. When it came time for the final exam, the professor merely put a chair up at the front of the room. He announced that the final exam was to prove that the chair did not exist. The students opened their examination booklets and feverishly started writing. After a minute, one student got up, turned his booklet in and left the room. All of the others kept writing until the test period was over. A week later the grades were posted. There was only one A given. Yes, it was the student who turned in the test so soon. The others wanted to know from him what he wrote. He exclaimed that he wrote only two words in the booklet -- *What chair?*

Sheila Levine was a beautiful and quite petite young lady. Long straight black hair framed a classic face accentuated by coal black eyes. Soft spoken and with clear diction, she greeted Parker cautiously. Her white blouse was neatly ironed and tucked into a plaid skirt. She presented a very positive first and lasting impression. When she sat across from him, the only telltale sign of a problem was how she so tightly clenched her hands in her lap.

He tried to put her at ease. "Autumn is my favorite time of year. The air is so sweet and fresh. It sort of coincides with the school year. It is a new beginning. It gives all of us a chance to start off invigorated and to create new experiences and adventures."

With a half smile she nodded, so he continued to make conversation. "I see you are majoring in Political Science. I could never get into that. But, I am sure you have not been enamored by any psychology courses you may have taken."

"I am going on to law school. I have wanted to be a lawyer as long as I can remember."

"That is wonderful. I have developed this philosophy which I suppose is psychologically based but it does seem to work out in general. I believe that young people are measured by how many dreams they collect. Old people, on the other hand, are gauged by how many dreams they have to give up. The real struggle, of course, is the in-between."

"I suppose I am a bit more practical than that. Being a lawyer is more than a dream. I rather pursue what I can see, what I can touch, than chase a dream." Her body appeared to relax, and her facial expressions revealed a charming animation as she spoke.

He forged ahead, setting the stage for the drama sure to follow. "I have always been a dreamer. A world of dreams can be a different form of reality. It at least can be a place to retreat to when harshness demands choices and we know it is too precarious to rush into action."

She inched up to the edge of the chair. "I have thought that the luxury of youth is to make choices, even if they are the wrong ones as long as we learn from those mistakes."

"It is not always easy to learn from a mistake."

"You must come across that scenario quite often. Can the fear of making a mistake cause the mistake or be a mistake itself?"

"It surely can be, I suppose, depending on what the mistake is going to be, how certain the prognosis of error, and just how consuming the fear is. A certain amount of apprehension can be a good thing, especially if it fine-tunes the experience. Do you like to talk in riddles?"

She was silent for a moment. "All of life, or our roles in it, as far as I can determine, is a riddle."

"True to a point. It can make a large difference if we are in the riddle as a player or merely an observer from afar."

She smiled slightly. "I hope I never come across an opposing attorney who is also a psychologist."

"Ah, and I hope that I never have to deal with another psychologist who is also a lawyer. So, tell me, young lady, a person who seems to have her feet on the ground and her sights on the gold ring, why do you need to talk to me?"

"I need someone to talk to who can be objective."

"I do try to be that. However, I am only human, with all of the weakness inherent in that condition. As I explain to others who come to see me, I do not make decisions for them. I will try to make you see things in a different light, consider options you may not have thought of, and offer the premise that for every problem there may be more than one solution."

"Sounds promising. What I tell you is in strict confidence, isn't it?"

"Yes, it would be because I believe in that. As a would-be

lawyer you will discover it is also protected by the law in what is called the doctor-patient privilege."

"Good." She feigned a smile, moved back in the seat, and crossed slim and shapely legs. "Just for background, you should know that I am Jewish. My parents are very, very religious. I could not see myself discussing my problem with a rabbi. My parents think that a rabbi knows all. I have tried talking to my friends but they fail to grasp the complexity of it for me. A problem for me is not a problem for them. They have faced a similar dilemma and the way has been untroubled for them, either because it is an isolated event or they do not attach the same kind of significance to it that I do."

Parker took the respite to offer her a glass of water. She took it, taking two quick swallows. Professionally, it was his turn to listen. This intelligent, well-spoken young woman already entranced him.

She continued, her eyes riveted to Parker's. "I suppose many people go to psychologists for sexual problems. Mine arises in part because of the strict religious upbringing I have had and in part because of my own beliefs which are antiquated by modern assessment. I want to be a virgin when I get married. I have a boyfriend here at Blantyre. We have been going together for almost a year. He is, fortunately, Jewish, but his family is far less strict than mine. He keeps pushing for sex. In all other respects, we get along fine. He keeps putting more and more pressure on me. My girlfriends think nothing about having sex with their boyfriends, and most think I am prudish. I really don't want to drop him. It is nice to have a steady and we do enjoy good times together. I am becoming a nervous wreck over this. Do you think I am crazy?"

Those alluring dark eyes were pleading for help. Parker stood up and went to the window staring out at the mountains.

He turned to her, speaking softly. "See those mountains standing firm and proud, braving every sort of dire element, and prevailing against all adversity? There is no way to describe that as crazy." He moved back to his chair at the desk.

With a quizzical look, she shot out at him, "Are you saying I should be stoic? I should be a mountain?"

"No. I cannot and should not tell you what to do. I merely point that out as one option. Mountains are a form of precedent for those who want to stand proud for what they do. This is your life, not mine. The one person, the only person, you must satisfy is the one you see in the mirror. To nearly every action there are short-term and long-term consequences. Look at and study the total picture. Listen to both your heart and your mind. You need to have a full understanding of yourself before you can really begin to fathom others. Project a year down the road, as an example. You will have graduated and gone on to law school. Is this fellow part of that scenario or is he merely the man of the moment?"

"How can a person tell how many options there are?"

"The options at both extremes, so to speak, are probably obvious. It is the possible array of choices in between that you need to grapple with. Not everything is black or white. I like to think that the same holds true for a yes or a no to a serious question. Can it be feasible to have a no or yes with conditions? Can there be a future yes or no? Can there be interim actions?"

"I thought I was supposed to ask the questions."

"You have as many answers as I do."

"I doubt that. I think you are just trying to show me that nothing is certain until I make it that way."

"Only you can do that."

She smiled, and it was a warm smile. "You're not much help. You are throwing me into the water to sink or swim."

He smiled back. "No, you are already in the water. You know you do not want to sink, you just need to know in which direction to swim, how fast, and to ward off other dangers that might lurk around you that are intent on seeing to it that you do not arrive at your destination."

She smiled again. "I thought you would talk in vagaries. Yet, I get the point. I already know that life itself is a form of vagueness and it is up to us to clarify our place in it. My answer may not correspond to others, and that will be alright."

"Precisely."

"Strange, I came here for answers. You haven't given me any but I feel better."

"Progress at the most rudimentary of levels."

"Would you mind if I came back another time to talk? Now that I think about it, there are very few people I can sincerely talk with. Roger, and that is his name, is one I converse with but don't really have the sense that we are talking."

"See how easy it can be to start on the road to finding your own answers."

"It is a revelation, not an answer."

"Still a piece of the solution puzzle."

He watched out the window as she walked from the building. Her raincoat was pulled tight against her slim frame. Her mind was probably running in high gear. She would make a fine lawyer, no doubt about that.

> *Happiness is not the absence of problems*
> *but the ability to deal with them.*
> Anonymous

FIVE

"How do you know the doc will like Greek chicken?"

Myrna smiled at Gabby. "He's not really a doctor, and who can resist my Greek chicken?"

"Doc suits him. Sounds better than mom's boyfriend."

"He is not my boyfriend either. We are just getting to know each other."

"You told me he kissed you. That makes him your boyfriend in my book. Maybe I will have a boyfriend some day."

"You will probably have more than I have ever had. We better hurry. He'll be here in fifteen minutes."

Gabby hastened her preparation of the salad plates. She sure did enjoy teasing her mother, and she thought how wonderful it was to see her so happy. If this doc could bring that kind of joy to her, he was great as far as she was concerned. Naturally, she was already far ahead of her mother, and by the end of this evening's dinner Gabby was going to decide if the doc might be a daddy for her.

Parker arrived, flowers in hand for Myrna and a book of verse for young folks for Gabby. Gabby squealed with delight, "I love poems."

Myrna chimed in as an afterthought, "And I love flowers. Thank you, kind sir."

The food and conversation were in abundance. Parker was most impressed with the mother-daughter interaction. Gabby was very polite, and she helped her mother without being asked to do so.

They sat in the living room after the meal, and had the dessert there. Myrna had made an apple pie, the local apples being plentiful at this time of the year. "Delicious," Parker offered as he sipped the accompanying hot chocolate.

"Mom is a great cook," Gabby interjected. "She would make a wonderful wife for some lucky man."

"That's a totally unbiased opinion," Myrna spoke in feigned strictness. "We sure were fortunate to have found this furnished house to rent. I especially like the kitchen. It is roomy and light. First pie I made in there, and it sure turned out good even if I have to say so myself."

Parker smacked his lips. "It is so good, and even though I shouldn't, I sure would like another small piece."

Gabby jumped to her feet. "I'll get it." Off she scampered into the kitchen.

Parker took advantage of her brief absence by going over to Myrna and kissing her softly on the cheek. "This has truly been a wonderful evening."

"You're not leaving yet, I hope."

"No. You can't get rid of me that easily. I am bursting with merriment and just had to vent it."

"Then you must also be a ventriloquist since you are speaking for me as well. Save some of your merriment for after Gabby goes to bed."

"Sure enough."

Gabby returned with the pie, and Parker accepted it gratefully. He devoured it as all eyes watched. "Mighty fine pie, and the service at this establishment is first rate."

Gabby giggled. "Mom, I hope you understand what he is saying."

Myrna joined in with laughter. "I'm not sure either. Maybe he wants another piece."

"No, thanks. I am stuffed," Parker interjected.

"Maybe it is just a clever way of trying to get invited over again."

"Now you are getting close."

Over the next couple of hours they played games. Gabby threw her arms around Parker and gave him a hefty hug just before Myrna took her up for bed.

In about twenty minutes Myrna returned. "For someone who has not had children of his own, you sure are good with them."

"You may not believe this but I was a child once. Thus, it is a natural talent. Of course, it is easy with her. She is pure delight, and that is all to your credit I am sure."

"I am not so sure. I read the parenting books, but they are really not any specific help. I think they just put parents at ease with the thought that problems are part and parcel of the growing years."

"Problems do not go away even after the growing years. The nature of the problems is different, that is all."

"Would you like some more hot chocolate?"

"No, not now. I would like you to sit close to me so I can whisper sweet nothings into your ear."

"No mortal woman can pass up an opportunity like that." She moved over to the sofa where he was sitting and sat very close to him, side touching side. She reached for his hand. "Whisper away."

"First, a whisper kiss."

"What kind of kiss is that?"

"A kiss so soft you can only hear in it whatever your heart desires."

"It better be a long one. My heart is filled with desire."

Gentle passion is no less amorous than robust desire.

Maturity may temper the tempo and intensity, yet the significance is as great and the dwelling in each emotional moment may actually be of greater impact. The whisper kiss spoke the sweet nothings through the lips. The nothings were in reality somethings.

Myrna checked to make sure Gabby was asleep. She then led Parker to her bedroom. She undressed him marveling at a male body still firm and youthful. His turn, and what he discovered belied her pronouncement of saggy and flabby. Her body was supple and warm. Whisper kisses ushered in a patient and gentle lovemaking. Myrna dared not open her eyes so the dream would not end. Parker dared not close his eyes for he did not want to forego a second of the reality he had sought for all this time.

You never lose by loving. You always lose by holding back.
Barbara De Angelis

SIX

Her dormitory window faced the mountains. As a senior she had managed to get this coveted single room. Opting out of joining a sorority, Alexa Wilson was a loner by choice and circumstance. Her depression grew daily. Being attractive and intelligent were not necessarily the ingredients for happiness. That lesson loomed large before her daily just as the majestic mountains dominated the horizon.

The one overriding memory of her childhood was the moment Aunt Celia, who was staying with her while her parents vacationed in France, told her that her parents had been killed in a plane crash. In that instant normal childhood had been snatched from her. The feeling of being alone, floating aimlessly in the world, took hold. To this day that feeling obscured any possible satisfaction she could derive from people or things.

At age nine, she had gone to live with that aunt. It was not the same as having her own parents. Aunt Celia was unmarried, brusque and unconcerned with her feelings. Alexa did not go hungry, and she did not want for any of the material things. Yet, her ego was never fed and her emotions never kindled. The concentration on not what she had but on what she was missing left her constantly sad and unfulfilled.

Here she was at Blantyre. As she entered the fourth year, majoring in English for the lack of any other choice that enticed her, she still had not the foggiest notion of what she wanted to do with her life. She could not even call it a life for that concept seemed so far removed from her grasp. She could not respond if one were to ask her who she was and what she was meant to be. Those were the issues that she raised with Parker Benson the three times she saw him last year. He had been reassuring, and his calm and steady voice soothed some of the outer fringes of her agitation. The words, however, were merely words with no connection to her reality. He had told her not to give herself any extra pressure. Much of her strain came from an impatience to find a path or pattern to her life. He told her it could come at any time. For some it is an arrival much later than wished for. He was the only one who cared about what she was going through. Little wonder that she had convinced herself that she was in love with him. Her sole comfort came in thoughts about him, thoughts that she jotted down in a notebook. Little tidbits of prose and poetry venting her feelings.

Even though she was not sure of herself, her intelligence aided in the analysis that she would most naturally fall in love with a man who had been kind to her. There are so few truly caring people in this world. That is as far as her intelligence could take her. Emotions, over which she seemed to have no control, would dictate what happens next.

Later, as she prepared to go for her appointment to see him, she dressed in her shortest skirt and tightest fitting sweater. If nothing else, he would notice her. Waiting to be announced by Arlene Peters, there was no doubt or hesitation in the plan she sought to carry out.

Parker went out to greet Alexa, strongly suspecting that he would have another session trying to assure her that she was not completely lost but had just not yet found her way. Her fetching outfit was not lost on him. He recalled a book he read some years back that stated that a woman who wore a tight sweater wanted men to appreciate her. Alexa was a beautiful and beguiling young woman. She had everything going for her, and he was surprised that young men were not falling over themselves trying to capture her heart. He had learned through many of such sessions that the elements of happiness do not necessarily bring such a result. Happiness is truly a state of mind, a contentment that is often generated merely because a person wants to be happy or, more urgently, does not want to be unhappy.

In the office, Alexa squirmed significantly in the chair, and before Parker could say a word she burst out in a high voice, "I love you."

Parker's response, even though taken a bit by surprise, was clinical. "I love you too, Alexa. We all need to love one another. The world would be a much better place if love prevailed."

As Alexa crossed her legs the short skirt hiked up considerably revealing full lovely thighs. "I don't mean it that way. I really am in love with you. I think about you all of the time."

Parker rose from his chair and sat on the corner of the desk close to her. He reached for her hand. She grasped it as if it was an act of desperation. "Alexa, I appreciate your strong feelings, and I am flattered to have a most beautiful young woman exclaim that she is in love with me. We are going to use that strong emotion to help you find the path to your own discovery of who you are and where you want to go in this life. It will be a challenge, no doubt about that. But I know you are up to it. Once you understand yourself you will know that there are many kinds of love. The love we share is based on our humanity. You want to be helped, and I want to help you."

A tear rolled down her cheek. "Please do not make fun of me."

Parker clenched her hand firmly. "Dear Alexa, believe me I am not making fun of you. I do not belittle the seriousness of these issues to you, and I know that they are painful. If it is serious to you, it is serious for me. Remember when we first chatted

I told you that I was your professional friend. The emphasis is on the word friend. I promise you that we are going to work through this together. I will not abandon you if you do not desert me."

She smiled sheepishly, "I wore this outfit to seduce you."

He placed his other hand over her clenched fingers, "You are beautiful, and very alluring. No man could resist such charms. Only a true friend can stand close and share those feelings in a different dimension. Part of who you are and who you will be is to reserve those delights for the special moments that accentuate their meaning."

"No wonder I love you. You make me feel good when I feel so bad. Does that make any sense?"

"It makes perfect sense. There is a certain affinity we feel towards those willing to help us. There is a reassurance of our own self worth and future when others will guide us. The one thing you should keep reminding yourself of is that you are not alone. Many others are also caught in that space between not knowing and wishing to know. It can be a vast void in that area between childhood and adulthood. That others wander there does not diminish the importance of it to you. You are not alone as long as you do not want to be alone. This is why you come to see me. We'll talk our way through your uncertainties. Just as long as you believe in yourself, just as I believe in you, you will find the answers to your questions. Maybe all of them will not be answered, and the answers may not come all at once, but they will come. I believe that. You must believe it as well."

"Why can't I make and keep friends?"

"Friendships will also come in time. Since you doubt yourself, you withhold yourself from others. When you distance yourself from others it is difficult for them to know you. There is no shame in admitting to others as you do to yourself that, for the lack of a better way to say it, you are neither here nor there. The people who can accept that, and many will because they see themselves in the same sort of dilemma, are your potential pool of friends. And then there will be a certain male who will capture your heart. Have you ever been in love?"

"Not really until you came along. From what I read, and the way Hollywood portrays it, you are my love."

"Again, you flatter me too much. I am not the god-like figure you imagine. Anyway, a time will come, perhaps even tomorrow, when you will meet a young man. The ripeness of the moment will be its own significance. The thrill will bring you new life. A mutually supportive relationship will grow, and it will be a mirror in which you can see yourself. Maybe, for the first time."

Alexa smiled and bent over and kissed the back of his hand. "You make it all sound so possible, but if it doesn't happen I don't think I can tolerate another disappointment. Maybe there are people who float in space all of their lives, and they never do land. I may be one of them."

Parker ached for this young person, so tormented by her own sense of unworthiness. "Alexa, all floaters land. Any simple act or occurrence can right your world in a flash. You will find yourself, and I just know you will like what you find."

"You make it all sound so appealing. In the meantime, I am going to suffer. Even the man I love has turned me down."

"I am not turning you down. I am just telling you I have a different role in your life. When you find yourself, you will know what I represent in your life."

"Are you allowed to hug me?"

"As a psychologist, no. As your professional friend, yes."

They hugged, and his nostrils filled with the vibrance of soap from her hair. Such a wonderful child. He just hoped her beautiful life materialized sooner rather then later.

When Alexa arrived back at her dormitory room, she sighed. Maybe if she thought he was beside her all of the time at least she might tolerate being a wanderer. She unfolded the piece of paper he had given her. A poem by Karen Ravn was hand-written on it:

> *Only as high as I reach can I grow,*
> *only as far as I seek can I go, only as*
> *deep as I look can I see, only as*
> *much as I dream can I be.*

SEVEN

By early November the winds were downright cold. Exposed areas of skin quickly became numb from the freezing temperatures. There had not yet been any measurable snow, although flurries and snow squalls were common. Even on the clear mornings as Parker trudged to his office, the expansive lawns cleaned of the fallen leaves, often had a heavy frost coating each blade. The early morning sun would glisten on the ice presenting a serene and almost magical panorama. Once again nature shows the beauty that can be created. Such are wondrous and endless masterpieces to admire.

As he walked along, he reflected on last night's dinner at Myrna's. The meals and quiet evenings had become a regular thing, and there was no doubt in his mind that he had a feeling of deep love for her. The relationship was satisfying, emotionally and physically. Myrna was a levelheaded, bright, and humorous person. She displayed a great sensitivity to all she observed and experienced. Her outlook on life was distinctly positive, and she radiated a calmness that affected all who came in contact with her. She was good for him, and he sensed that he was all she sought in a companion. He was so fond of Gabby that he already considered her as a daughter.

For Myrna, this was a true connection. Parker was the love of her life. She could see that now, comparing it to her poor choice of a mate before. His gentleness and consideration captivated her. That he was so good with Gabby was a definite plus. So far, Parker had satisfied her every physical and emotional need. Little wonder that she basked in a complete happiness that was denied to her for so long.

Neither one brought up the subject of the future. It was as if there was an implied understanding that they would take it a day at a time. Maturity is its own temperance.

The one item that was discussed was the plan for the soon to arrive Thanksgiving break. Myrna and Gabby were to go to her brother's house in Virginia. She suggested that Parker join them, but he declined feeling that it was a time for them to be with their family and it was too soon for him to meet any relatives. Since he would be going to Florida over the Christmas leave to spend that time with his sister, he would just stay here and enjoy some quiet time. He was already behind in writing and filing his reports, and it would be an opportune time to catch up on this drudgery. Myrna was tempted to cancel the travel plans so they might be together. She did not want him to spend the holiday alone. However, she thought better of it just to let things proceed naturally and not to push it. Still from the old school, it might well be interpreted that things were quite serious to bring a man home for a holiday with the family. As far as she was concerned it was serious, but she was not yet up to all of the discussions and explanations.

As he walked to the office that early November morning, even the winter coat, wool cap and gloves were inadequate against the cold. It would have been cozy to have stayed at home, reading and drinking hot chocolate. He had a busy schedule for the day, so the thought was soon carried off in a gust of wind.

His first patient of the morning was a freshman, Drake Longwood. The intriguing description on the questionnaire read: *sibling rivalry*. Drake was in the School of Liberal Arts, and in the first year a major is not yet selected.

When Drake entered Parker's office, his step was tentative. Small in stature, he had a long drawn face with glasses riding low on a narrow nose. There was a slight stutter to his speech. "Dr. Benson, is it alright for me to come in? There was no one out front."

"Arlene must have stepped out. Sure, if you are Drake this is your appointed hour. Come in, please. Close the door, sit and make yourself comfortable."

After sitting, Drake diverted his eyes so he did not have to make eye contact. "I am not too comfortable coming to see you. I am not even sure anyone can help me."

"I am not here to help you. My only design is through conversation that you perhaps can find a way to help yourself. We'll just talk. Everything said in this office is strictly private. No one will ever know from me what you were here about. Many students come to see me just to talk. I like to think I am an objective listener. There are times that things people harbor within themselves emerge in some manageable form when discussed. You will find no pressure here. No judgments are made. You can say as much or as little as you are comfortable with. You can talk to me just this one time or as many times that you feel warranted. In this place, contrary to what prevails outside of these walls, I am a person who will listen intently to whatever you say. There are not enough true listeners in the world. Apparently, few are willing to exert the effort and give up the time to actually listen."

Drake frowned. "I read somewhere that in reality we only hear what we want to hear."

"That is probably true generally. Those who have their own agenda stretch to hear confirmation of their side, or they are so intent on formulating what they will say next that all of the words spoken by others do not register with them. An objective listener does not have to confirm or deny his beliefs in the process."

"Do you ever get tired of listening to the problems of others?"

"I never would have gone into this profession if I thought listening brought burdens. The stark reality is that everyone has problems, some more than others, and some more pressing than others. If I can gain the confidence of my patients, my reward is sharing insights into their problems. I am not a magician and do not claim to perform miracles. Experience teaches that most problems are best met head on. There is an Italian saying to the effect that if there is a monster in your life, first you try to overcome him. If that does not work then you invite him to dinner."

"There is a definite type of monster in my life, but I am not sure it isn't me."

"What makes you think you are your own monster?"

"I am not sure I can adequately describe it."

"Just talk about it. Let's see what crops up."

Drake shuffled his feet, and Parker was sure he noted a tear in the corner of his eye. His discomfort was either being here or with himself, or both. "Envy is consuming me. Maybe it has already consumed all of me. I have an older brother that I have had to compete with all of my life. Our parents, relatives, friends, neighbors, all compare me to him, and I always come out on the short end. He excels in everything. He is athletic, handsome, and witty. I pale in his shadow. He is the perfect son, and our parents favor him. He has received the attention, the gifts, and girls fall at his feet. On top of it all, he is really a great guy. I try to hate him but he is so damned nice that I wind up hating myself. Everyone admires and respects him. In contrast, I am mediocre. Athletics and intellectual endeavors are a struggle. The only girls that have ever paid attention to me are the ones who hope to get close to my handsome brother through me. My inferiority complex is well founded, believe me. I am very unhappy and just do not know what to do about it. So, here I am. Talking about it hasn't helped. It just accentuates my misery. I hate me and what I have become."

Parker rose, walked towards him, and sat on the corner of the desk. "Sounds like a pretty good description of your monster. Time to do battle to overcome the beast. If that fails, you can invite him to dinner."

Drake gritted his teeth. "What does that mean exactly?"

"It means you have to rid yourself of the emotional burden or learn to live with it."

"Just how do I drive it out of my life? It has been such a pervasive element in my growing years. It is me."

"First, to state the obvious. It is not simple. It is not an overnight catharsis. No one can do it for you. You know the nature of the beast and you have the ability to slay it. Just our talk here leads me to conclude that you are a bright and worthwhile person in your own right. Somehow you have to convince yourself that your self worth is separate and distinct from your brother's. You are who you are as a person and not just your brother's brother. Walk in the sunlight by yourself and there will be no shadow but your own. People are complex and simple at the same time. Some are more of this, and some are less of that. Each of us is different, and just that difference can be a major asset. Our place in the scheme of things is what we basically make of it on our own. If we do not become a President, a corporate executive, a star football player, or a movie star, the life we make for ourselves can be just as important. It can be just as meaningful and rewarding in a different way. One secret is not to look over your shoulder to see where you have been. Look ahead to a point you would like to be at. Pride and satisfaction in that journey can bring your own happiness. That is the cornerstone of a sustainable life. Somewhere out there is a woman who will love you for who you are. She will accept your brother for who he is, mainly on the ground that he is your brother, part of your family. But, her love will be for you alone. Your life never did have to parallel that of your brother's. Your roads are separate, and your destinations not necessarily the same. Despite his attributes, your humanity is equal. What you do with that will define your life and will delineate your future. Your monster, the ghosts of your past, can be left behind whenever and wherever you deem it to happen."

Drake sighed. "You make it sound so plausible."

"It is worth your best shot, isn't it?"

"Yes. How do I begin?"

"You already have. The vehicle of Drake is the one for you to drive, to steer, and to shift gears. You can change its direction at your will. We can talk whenever you want to. I am your sounding board. Your ideas and your actions are your self portrait."

"I guess this is a beginning of sorts. Frankly, I do not feel any better about me. I do feel some relief that I have been able to talk about my predicament. I also like knowing that someone else knows. But, what do I do now?"

Parker's empathy reached out to all of these troubled youngsters. If only he could physically guide them and lead them to a place where their minds could settle on positive thoughts. Yet, they really had to stumble along on their own. That was truly the way for them to gain satisfaction. "You probably need to see how the dust of this talk settles. Take a long walk and mull over what you have said and our discussion. Let the concepts sink in. Try to be upbeat about what the future may hold for you. At times, the slightest change in outlook can make a big difference. Immerse yourself in your studies because the better you do here at Blantyre, the better you will feel about yourself overall."

As Drake closed the door behind him, he was glad he had

gone to see the good doctor. The things he had heard about him turned out to be true. The one point that stayed with him so strongly was that he needed now to concentrate on himself and not on his brother. He followed the advice and took a long walk. He saw things along the way that he swore he had not seen before. There had to be some significance to that.

Parker sat back in his chair. One of the tragic elements of life for young people is that no one listens to them. A truly caring parent or friend could do many of the things he does as a professional. Where are they?

Be yourself, everyone else is already taken.
Oscar Wilde

EIGHT

Unforeseen events can take control of a situation, sending even the soundest of plans askew. Just was this the case when the nor'easter hit the East Coast with relentless harshness from Virginia up to New England just the day before the Blantyre Thanksgiving break was to begin. Over a two-day period, the University was buried by more than two feet of snow with no prospect of letting up. Transportation was at a standstill, and nearly everyone's plans were affected. While the dorms were not scheduled to close, the school cafeterias were to be shut. Now, they scrambled to remain open with short supplies and staff. Students, teachers and administrative personnel had to cancel homeward bound trips. Myrna's trip had to be cancelled from both ends. Her family in Virginia was snowbound too. They would be spending the Holiday with Parker after all. A strange turn of events to engage the mind.

Parker had previously bought a roasting chicken to have on Thanksgiving. He packed it in plastic, and trudged through the snow on the hike to Myrna's house. There was no sense in trying to dig the car out. Myrna had some food in the house but was glad to see the chicken. That was the closest they would get to a turkey meal. If only they did not lose electricity so they could get it cooked. On the porch, she and Gabby brushed the layers of snow off his coat and cap. The items were hung up to dry in the storeroom. In spite of the weather, they had much to be thankful for this Thanksgiving. Brought together by the elements, the sense of warm closeness enfolded them.

The giant snowstorm also altered plans for others, and such adjustments can be difficult. When plans are set, expectations arise. Not meeting those expectations can either bring disappointment or a reprieve.

Alexa Wilson could not see the mountains from her dormitory window as the snow was falling so heavily and blowing around in all directions. Being here was a mixed blessing. She was spared from a frosty few days with Aunt Celia. She had made reservations at a restaurant for Thanksgiving dinner. There was no feeling of family, no bond of unity. Alexa would not have to embellish stories just to hold her aunt's interest during their limited conversations.

Her mind often raced beyond her capacity to fully reason. Dr. Benson must also be stuck here. Teacher and staff addresses were confidential, but she suspected he might live in the faculty housing up on the hill. Maybe his name would be on the mailboxes, or on the door, so if she went from unit to unit she might luckily locate him. He would have to let her in from the storm. She would then pour on the charm and crack his resistance. She wanted to sacrifice her virginity to this caring man, knowing in her heart that he would be gentle and protective of her. Love can be reassuring even in the midst of undaunted imagination.

Pondering for a moment what sort of excuse she might come up with to explain why she would be looking for him, she sat down at her desk and started to write a poem. She would exclaim that she just could not wait to share it with him.

My Enemy is Loneliness

How come I am alone even in a crowd?
How come no one hears me when I shout aloud?

Why in the mirror is there no defined reflection?
Why does my mind support my heart's deception?
        Why is there question after question?

My growth is painful and troubled,
Steeped in turmoil when efforts are doubled;
Carried in the wind are my cries of despair,
No one to listen, no one willing to share.
        No answers, no solace, and no one to care.

Does one resolve to go alone through each day?
Can there be another that can show the way?
If there is no destination, which way to walk?
When always alone to whom do I talk?
        More questions, more answers sought.

One man stands on the high plateau smiling,
With a manner comforting, a form so beguiling;
Can he feel the love that I have for him?
The only true solution to my life so grim.
        Hear me well, my love, this is no whim!

Alexa's thoughts vaulted across boundaries both real and imaginary. Evil designs emerged shocking her to the core. After all, she could coerce Parker's attention towards her by threatening to go public with accusations of concocted sexual advances made by him. As quickly as they reared their ugly head, she dismissed them with a loud grimace. The one thing she was sure about herself was that she was a decent person. In her quest to find herself she could not and would not live a lie. She also admired Dr. Benson for his respectful and genuine concern about her plight. That would not be jeopardized by a web of deceit. If she could not win his love as the person she hoped to be, the victory would be meaningless.

With the poem tucked in snuggly beneath the layers of sweaters and a bulky coat, she set out on her trek. The snow was blinding, and it whipped against her face. Fitting the scarf over her face so only her eyes were exposed, the snow quickly froze on her eyelashes. After making short progress, her intelligence overrode her emotions and she turned back to the dormitory. She would make an appointment to see him when classes resumed. The poem would be delivered then, and he would not be able to deny her love.

Sheila Levine looked out at the blizzard, feeling relieved that she did not have to go home for the break. She loved her parents dearly, and was grateful for the secure home environment that their religious ways fostered. Yet, now it was restricting to her. The reality of the world, and the impact of the ingrained and growing desire to be a lawyer gradually led her to shun the confines of the religious past. The dogmas had lost their luster. The ethical aspects would carry forth in her profession and future life. The virginity goal also loomed large in her personal composite. It was an unshakeable principle. Breaking up with Roger was easy to do once that decision was made. Upon reflection, he was too shallow for her and her wanting the companionship was the deception of the reality. Wanting compatibility can easily trick the mind into believing it exists. With that demanding pressure for sex removed from her realm, her resolve in the various directions of her being strengthened even more.

Now, she actually felt quite good about herself. There was a display of determination in her convictions. No longer a sheep to potentially follow the flock, she proudly stood head and shoulders above the crowd. She defied commonality and would be her own person. She would make an appointment with the good doctor so she might flaunt this firmly established self-commitment. She would employ the mountain analogy that he had pointed out to her. Her announcement would be that she had peaked.

The first thought Drake Longwood had when it was finalized that the students would not be able to go home for the holiday was that his parents would not even realize that he was not there. After all, they had Phil. With a shake of his head he thought better of it. He had to stop being so negative about himself. If he did not think highly of himself, nobody else would either. It would be just a few weeks to the Christmas break, and he could use that time to work on putting everything into perspective. Acceptance was the key to his future. He doubted that he could subdue the monster, but if he learned to live with him gradually the beast might go away. There was enough room in his heart to love his brother as well as himself. It all sounded so good in theory, and it seemed so plausible when removed from the home environment. Christmas would be the first true test.

A postponement of sorts was not what Richard Clemmons wanted. He talked to Laura every night on the telephone, sometimes for hours. He listened intently as she poured her heart out to him. He was hoping that when he saw her over the holiday he might formulate a decision on how to proceed with the relationship. Each time he thought it best for both of them to break it off, doubts and misgivings arose as they talked. Not only were her feelings for him so strong, as she expressed them so often and in various ways, he also found himself looking forward to their conversations. Gradually, she led him to talk more and more about his own needs and desires. There was a definite bond between them and he was not sure the tragedy affected that. The truth of the matter was that he had no idea how he would react when he saw her. However, he was anxious to resolve it, and this delay would only increase his anxiety. His sigh was long. One more unknown to have to live with.

> *If the mind is to emerge unscathed from the relentless struggle with the unforeseen, two qualities are indispensable: first, an intellect that, even in the darkest hour, retains some glimmerings of the inner light which leads to the truth; and second, the courage to follow this light wherever it may lead.*
> Karl von Clausevitz

NINE

Myrna had to read the letter from her attorney three times before the full significance of it sunk in. Just when things were going so well in her life, the past emerges to haunt her being. Her ex-husband, George, was threatening to bring an action to get full custody of Gabby based on Myrna's unilateral removing her from the jurisdiction of Virginia and jeopardizing his visitation rights. Even though he had not made any attempt to see or otherwise communicate with Gabby for years, her attorney speculated that this was merely a ploy for George to get out of having to pay child support anymore. He opined that the attempt was groundless but that she should prepare herself for a hearing if George pushed the matter. Any prospect of her losing Gabby, no matter how remote, shook her to the core.

Parker was completely supportive, just as she surmised he would be. He even offered to go down with her if the hearing ever took place. She pulled out her copy of the divorce agreement, and there was nothing in it dealing with her moving out of Virginia. George was granted visitation rights if he requested them and Myrna agreed to any proposed visit. Otherwise, it merely provided that George was to pay an amount monthly for support of Gabby until she reached the age of eighteen or Myrna remarried.

It was arranged that Myrna would meet with her attorney while she was in Virginia during the Christmas break. In the meantime, she was upset and it distracted from her present happiness. She told Gabby all about it. There had been no secrets, and there was no reason she should not know what was going on. Gabby's father was a stranger, and from her point of view she did not care to have anything to do with him. Her mother was her entire world, with the prospect of letting the doc into the charmed circle.

Snowdrifts were still piled high but a week of bright sunshine left the streets and walkways clean and dry. The University had been in a state of suspended animation since the Thanksgiving shut down, and students and staff seemed to be just biding their time before the exodus for the Christmas holiday.

Alexa waited anxiously at Dr. Benson's office. She watched Arlene Peters intently as the woman efficiently fielded phone calls while still working on the computer. Alexa wondered if she could ever reach a place of settlement where she could concentrate on more than one task at a time. Would she arrive at a point where she might feel satisfaction from doing a job?

As she waited, she went over in her mind just how she was going to handle the delicate situation with the man she loved. Just then Drake Longwood rushed into the building and up to Arlene's desk. Evidently quite agitated, he exclaimed, "I must see Dr. Benson right away."

Arlene gazed intently at him recognizing a danger sign, "Do you have an appointment?"

"No," he shouted. "Please just tell him that Drake Longwood is here and must see him, even for just a couple of minutes."

Motioning over to Alexa's direction, Arlene said with a bit of sternness, "He has someone with him right now and this young lady has been waiting for a good time and she is next. Why don't you sit down and I will talk to Dr. Benson to see what might be done."

Drake shuffled over to a chair near where Alexa was sitting. He glanced at the beautiful young woman and wondered how she could have any problem that would need psychological assistance. To his surprise, his breathing became calmer. He just could not keep his eyes off the girl's majestic face. Her tight sweater revealed substantial breasts, and the short skirt offered a view of shapely legs.

Alexa noticed how this geekish fellow was gawking at her. She tried to concentrate on her plan but the situation became rather uncomfortable. "Do you enjoy staring at others?"

Somewhat taken aback, as if he had been undetectable in his private thoughts, he stammered, "I'm sorry. You are just the most beautiful girl, so beautiful I can't take my eyes off of you. Makes me mad that I rushed out of my dorm room without cleaning my glasses. I don't want to miss a blemish, even if you had one."

"Only a lowly freshman would say such a stupid thing."

A put down was common in his world. "Is the emphasis on *fresh* or *man*? "

She appraised him anew, and the more she gazed upon him his gawky looks and actions were in a way refreshing. So used to artificiality, he now came across to her as being genuine. "Why do you have to see the doc so urgently?"

"It is a long, long story. An unforeseen crisis is emerging. Why does someone so lovely, a goddess if I might add, have to see him at all?"

"In my case it is a foreseen crisis emerging."

Meanwhile, Arlene had interrupted Parker in the session with another student, an action reserved for the most serious of events. Parker said he was almost finished and would come out to talk to them to try and work out something. He sensed that Drake's urgency was greater than Alexa's but that her fragility could easily be wounded.

"I have never been called a goddess before," Alexa smiled. "Sounds good if it also has great powers attached to it."

Drake found himself growing calmer. The agitation that had gripped him was fading away. "If you had great powers, what would you do with them?"

"That's not the kind of question I can answer without thinking about it. Initially, I suppose, I would be torn between wanting to do some good for all people and being selfish and wanting to right my own life."

"Your life cannot possibly be as haywire as mine."

"Your problems probably pale compared to mine."

Parker and Arlene came out of the office. Parker looked at the two troubled youths before him, and he hoped the suggestion would be accepted. "Alexa, would you mind if I met with Drake for a few moments first? I'll tag on extra time for you at the end of the session."

Alexa nodded, and Drake followed Parker into the office. The student that had been in the office must have left by the side door.

When settled, Parker noticed that Drake appeared more at ease than Arlene had described. "Well, Drake, what has upset the apple cart?"

"I know you are busy, and perhaps I shouldn't have bothered you. Strangely, I am not as upset about it now as I was a while ago. The postponement of seeing my family to Christmas gave me a good opportunity to plan out just what I would say, just what I would do. Then last night, my brother called. His team is coming to Blantyre on Saturday to play our team in basketball at the gym. He asked me to come to the game and to have dinner with him afterwards. It caught me by surprise and laid all of my plans on end."

"If you think about it, actually it might be good to face him without the rest of the family around, especially on your own turf. You'll be in control and can pick the restaurant."

"There won't be time to go to a restaurant, since their bus will be leaving two hours after the game. By the time he showers, the cafeteria will be the only place to go to."

"Better yet. It is your cafeteria, a place you frequent every day."

"Yes, I can see that this might be a good thing. It will either add to my resolve or set me back."

"Why not just concentrate on it as fortifying you as an individual meeting with another individual who just happens to be your brother."

Drake stood up and turned to go. "I suppose I should have figured this out for myself. It is comforting to know you are here."

"Good luck. I am confident all will end just fine."

Drake emerged from the office and smiled at Alexa. He sat down next to her. "Alexa is such a nice name. It fits you."

"Thanks," she said softly. "You weren't in there long. Just confirms that my problems are greater."

"Time and attention do not necessarily indicate gravity."

"Especially without an appointment."

Drake laughed, further putting him at ease. "Would you mind if I waited here for you. Maybe we can take a walk."

Alexa looked at the young man, and she saw so much more than her first impression. Any geekishness was transformed by a warm smile and an endearing mannerism. "Sure, I would like that."

Parker opened the office door and motioned for Alexa to come in. He noticed Drake sitting there. Perhaps two wanderers had crossed paths, as sometimes that does happen.

Alexa clutched her coat as she sat across from Parker. The

poem was in a pocket of the coat. Her plan was to give it to him and then throw herself at him when he finished reading it. Her mind willed her to reach into the pocket and fetch the paper but her hand did not move.

"Can I hang the coat up for you?" Parker sensed a tension in the young woman's posture.

She offered it to him without retrieving the poem. A momentary catharsis, triggered by meeting Drake, and she was unable to speak.

He smiled warmly. "Have you met Drake?"

She nodded, and he continued. "Generally, I try not to let my patients meet one another. Worthy events can emerge from accidental meetings. We have talked about that before. Around the next corner or beyond the next rise in the road can be an answer."

She smiled, and he observed how truly beautiful she is. A clear complexion, wide eyes and delicate features. All of the wonders of life at her doorstep. All she had to do was to reach out for it.

His observation was interrupted when her soft voice began. "I have had a revelation of sorts. It does not answer any of my questions, and it certainly does not change my limbo status. Yet, I have found out a few things about myself, things that I take pride in and that comfort me. Basically, I know for sure that I am a decent human being. I will not live by a falsehood. I will not gain an advantage by deceit or by hurting someone else. I have also just discovered that if I want to I can see beyond what my first sight reveals to me. That way I can discover things that others may not see. A good start, wouldn't you say?"

Parker beamed. "Yes, a terrific start, Alexa. I am real proud of you. You have just gained a glimpse of the life you deserve for yourself."

They talked for a long time. Alexa had forgotten all about the poem, and all about seducing Parker. She hugged him before she left but it was not an amorous hug. It was the grasp of gratitude. Some of the seeds he had planted were bearing fruit. She could now believe in herself because he had started that trip by believing in her.

Drake was waiting for her. They walked and talked for about an hour. The cold had gotten to them so they stopped at the cafeteria for coffee, and each went off to a class. They planned to meet again for dinner. For two friendless people, unsure of themselves and uncertain about tomorrows, they shared a bond that prompted a real chance for new horizons.

A friend is a gift you give yourself.
Robert Louis Stevenson

TEN

Gabby was sound asleep. There is nothing quite like the undisturbed sleep of the young and innocent. Myrna's sleep was restless, and even with Parker's arms around her she realized that she was not at peace with herself as she had thought. Parker sensed her uneasiness, and he clenched her even closer as if that would make her pain go away. He left before Gabby awoke. They did not want her to know just yet that he stayed most of the night on many occasions.

Myrna could still feel his gentle kiss on her lips as she sipped her coffee. She could not lose this man just as she could never give Gabby up. She needed him to make her feel whole.

Gabby came into the kitchen dressed for school. She sat at the table and started on the breakfast that was waiting for her. Her mother was always there for her. It was now important that she be here for her. "Mom, are you worried about the custody thing?"

"Yes, sweetie, I am. I can't help it. You are just so precious to me."

"Nobody can take me away. I want to be with you forever."

"That is comforting, dear. We probably shouldn't be concerned about it. We cannot let it detract from our life here. You concentrate on school as if nothing has happened."

"I'll try. I really will. You need to promise me that you will not let it interfere with you either, especially with the doc."

"You like him don't you?"

"Yes. Probably as much as you do."

"I love him."

"I know."

"Would it be alright with you if he came to live with us as soon as we get this custody matter straightened out once and for all?"

"Would you marry him?"

"If he asks me, I would accept on the spot if I knew you were comfortable with it."

"I just want you to be happy. Having the doc here all the time would be cool."

Myrna hugged her small frame close to her. There was no way she could stop the tears. Gabby was her extended self and a delight in her own way.

Alexa and Drake had dinner together all week. On Friday night, Alexa offered to go with Drake to the game the following day. Drake was ecstatic. He had let this girl get closer to him than anybody else had. He spoke freely to her of all of the things that troubled him. His private reserve of doubts was opened. For Alexa, Drake was an alter ego. It mattered not that he was two years younger. She considered him her equal intellectually and emotionally. She did not hesitate to bare her inner most thoughts. When they talked, reactions and impressions reached a common ground.

"Do you think a man and woman can just be friends?":

Alexa pondered the question for a moment. "I really don't know. We'll find out, won't we?"

What was even more revealing for Drake was the absence of any apprehension of what might happen if Alexa met Phil. Nothing could penetrate the friendship they had discovered. He was more confident about that than he was about himself. In a matter of days, Alexa had done for him what he had been unable to do himself. Dr. Benson had left out an option. Drake did not have to slay the monster or invite him to dinner. He could find someone who could devour the monster for him.

The game on Saturday was one-sided just as everyone expected. Blantyre never touted itself as an athletic powerhouse. Alexa and Drake had a good time cheering the team on anyway. Alexa's only comment when Drake pointed Phil out on the court was that beneath the baggy shorts he had cute legs.

After the game, Alexa waited with Drake for Phil to shower and change into street clothing. Drake wanted her to go with them for dinner, but she told him it would be better for him to go alone. She did agree to meet Phil. Now that she knew all of the details of Drake's torment, she agreed with Dr. Benson's suggestion that it would be best if he faced his past and present on his own. That would set his future free.

Drake introduced them, and Alexa kissed Drake on the cheek wishing them a nice dinner. An extra squeeze on Drake's arm was not lost on him.

As they headed for the cafeteria, Phil remarked, "Alexa is a beautiful girl."

"She is that, inside as well."

"Are you two dating?"

Drake was tempted to embellish the facts, perhaps showing Phil that he too could charm a beauty. He knew deep down that his climb to an equal plateau had to be based on honesty. That was a lesson instilled by Dr. Benson and reinforced by Alexa. "We are just very good friends. Romance would get in the way of that."

"You are lucky there my brother. None of the girls I get involved with can hold a steady conversation."

A shy smile crossed Drake's lips. "You need to see beyond the obvious. It took some learning on my part. It is definitely a trait worth developing."

Here he was telling his older, smarter, handsomer brother how to live life. Some moments can truly be sweet.

The dinner and accompanying conversation were uneventful. Drake saw him off at the team bus, returned to his dorm room and telephoned Alexa. He described his emotional victory. Her reaction was animated. "I'm happy for you, dear Drake. Maybe it will fortify me to deal with my aunt on an honest level."

"I do hope so. How obvious and simple it is when you experience it. People must accept you for who you are. If they do not do that, let them deal with it."

"I guess I need to call you Mr. Wisdom from now on."

"Drake Wisdom has a nice ring to it. Dr. Benson opened my eyes, but you have swiveled my head so I can see my total surroundings. I like what I see."

"The best part, dear friend, is that I see through your eyes as well. A world is out there for me too."

"I wish you were here so that I could hug you."

"I feel it through the phone. Can you feel my arms around you?"

"I do. I am saving a special embrace for you when I see you tomorrow."

"Ditto. Good night dear heart."

"Thank you. Have wonderful dreams."

When there is no enemy within,
the enemies outside cannot hurt you.
African proverb

ELEVEN

The Christmas break snuck up on the Blantyre University community sooner than most realized. With the weather cooperating, those intending to depart did so, some earlier than others.

Sheila Levine's plan was to go home early for a few days, and then she would visit with her Aunt Sarah in Connecticut. Since there was no Christmas to celebrate in her Jewish household, and Yom Kippur came early this year, she would concoct a reason to visit her aunt. Assistance with her studies seemed most plausible. Aunt Sarah, her father's sister had been an outcast from the family. Not pursuing Jewish ways, she had become famous in her own right as a documentary writer for television. Admiring intellectuals, her parents had softened their opinion about Sarah over the years and while they would not embrace her into the fold, they did not protest too strongly about Sheila's impending visit. Sarah, for her part, had always taken a special interest in Sheila, recognizing a superior intelligence and a robust rebelliousness to match her own. She had convinced her brother to let Sheila come for a visit to help soothe her emotional aftershock from a failed marriage while also helping the younger child with academic matters. Her paying Sheila's transportation eased the way, particularly since her house was quite near the train station.

When Richard Clemmons arrived back at his Long Beach home, his parents were slightly miffed that he rushed out of the home grabbing the family car keys, but they knew their son had not yet resolved the situation with that troubling girl. They hoped he would settle things once and for all so that they might have a peaceful and joyous family holiday. Richard, with a refreshingly open mind, awaited the result of whether the waters were to be calm or calamitous.

While Laura Draggond waited for Richard, her thoughts and desires had undergone quite a metamorphosis over the past few weeks. Placing her mother's suicide in some form of rationalized position in relation to her own state of well being, she realized that her feelings for Richard were more of a reaction to that terrible happening than out of her personal emotional need. Richard was convenient to hold on to when everything else was falling apart. It was a purely selfish reaction. Richard was on a different life plan than she was. He was in college, and destined to be a professional. She, on the other hand, really had ordinary and less heightened expectations. Free from her mother's yoke, the clerical job she obtained at the insurance company was about as fulfilling as she had a right to demand. Richard was there when she needed and wanted someone, his initial image as a lifeguard enhancing a young girl's imagination and fancy. Now, it was clear that she had to prove to herself that she could stand on her own two feet, needing no one but herself until the dream she harbored since a little girl of marriage and family closed in on her.

They drove to one of the beach entries, now isolated and secluded in winter's grasp. Parked in the darkness, Laura explained her feelings, perhaps not as eloquently as she had hoped for but the gist of her message was clear. They embraced and Richard pronounced to always be available if she needed to talk. Both knew that this would be the last contact. A tomorrow can be lost when today consumes it.

When Richard arrived back at the house, the turn of events

elated his parents. He was not quite sure how he felt. It seemed odd that what had appeared to be such a complex situation could be resolved so simply, so quickly. Later that night as he lay in bed trying to sleep, the full significance of Laura's gift to him became evident. She was after all quite a wonderful person and he was glad that he had stuck with her to ease the transition from tragedy to self-reliance. In the final analysis, she had given more to him than he had to her. The significance of the lesson would no doubt stay with him all of his life.

Alexa also had difficulty falling asleep the first night at her aunt's apartment. They had clashed, as she knew they would. Excited about having Drake as a friend, she had blurted it out and Aunt Celia had interpreted it all wrong. She castigated Alexa for getting involved with a younger boy, heaping all of the staid clichés on her as if following a script. Tempers flared, and a chill descended to match the dreary cold of the winter's shroud. Alexa decided she would stick it out for the couple of days to Christmas and then return early to the campus telling her aunt that she still needed to work on research papers. Fortunately, the dorms were open, and she would just have to eat at the restaurants in town.

Drake entered his home as a new person. Coming off the emotionally successful encounter with his brother, and having Alexa as his stalwart friend, he accepted and treated his parents with a new maturity. They must have sensed the change in him as they engaged him in conversation frequently and were more inclined to include him in all of the family holiday preparations. He felt bolder and wiser. When Alexa informed him on the telephone of her plan to return to school early, it was a natural decision for him to do the same and to meet her there.

Myrna stood before her brother's house, put her arm around Gabby, and uttered quietly, "Sweetie, wherever we are together, it is home. This is our home for the holiday. Let's have fun and forget about other difficulties."

Gabby looked up at her. "I wish the doc was with us."

"So do I. So do I."

Myrna remembered the previous night when she clutched at Parker with ardent passion. There was no need for words. His fingers walked along her body, and her ecstasy ascended. The separation was going to be trying, especially with the dreaded meeting with her attorney looming ahead. She was stronger now than she had ever been. She would get through this, and nothing would change for the worse. She would get to a point where she would look back into the shadows knowing that whatever lurked there would stay there.

> *The reason people find it so hard to be happy is*
> *that they always see the past better than*
> *it was, the present worse than it is, and*
> *the future less resolved than it will be.*
> Marcel Pagnol

TWELVE

One of the greatest mysteries and challenges of life is when an unanticipated development stops you dead in your tracks. It can pull the rug out from under your feet leaving you unsettled in the clear path you thought you were taking. There would be no way of knowing whether you might land head or feet first. Your direction can be intrepidly changed. Parker was to experience this for himself.

He had driven to the airport in Boston as the closest one he could get a nonstop flight to St. Augustine, Florida, where his sister Clarisse lived. It promised to be a comforting time to spend a couple of weeks with his kindly sister. There would be much to catch up on. He had told her about Myrna and Gabby but was keeping the savory details for a quiet time when they would be sitting on Clarisse's porch overlooking the bay.

As he made his way down the plane to his aisle seat, he noticed that there were few empty seats. Florida is a popular holiday and winter destination. Matching his ticket with the seat, a very attractive woman was sitting in the middle seat with a young girl occupying the window seat. The girl looked about Gabby's age, and she smiled broadly at Parker.

Parker tucked his briefcase under the seat before him and buckled the seat belt. He turned toward the woman next to him, again enthralled by her fine looks. The clarity of her complexion was striking. "Tucked in and ready for flight."

The woman smiled warmly, and spoke in a mellow and clear voice, "Nap time already?"

"Any time can be nap time. Let me introduce myself. I am Parker Benson."

"I am Rhona Kingsley. And this is my daughter, Francine, but you better call her Franny."

"Off to Florida on a vacation?"

"Not quite. My elderly parents live in St. Augustine at a nursing home and we spend each Christmas with them there."

"I am visiting my sister who lives there. Our parents died in a nursing home there last year."

"Sorry," her voice softening and a warm look filled her clear dark eyes.

"It is not a comforting part of life to have older folks who need special care and who depend on you."

She glanced quickly out of the window before looking directly at him. "I am learning that first-hand. Mom and dad are failing perceptively. It is more shocking as I see them so little. If I saw them every day I might understand it better. Now, it is heart-wrenching."

"Is your husband joining you there?"

"Not likely. We have been divorced for five years. Is your wife catching up with you?"

"I have never been married. What do you do when you are up north?"

"I am a professor of psychology at Ellenshire College, a small women's school just outside of Boston."

"I have heard of it. It has a fine reputation. Coincidentally, I am the University Psychologist at Blantyre University."

She grinned. "It can be a small world."

He smiled broadly. "Yes, it sure can."

Rhona placed her hand over Franny's small fingers. It was her way of reassuring her that this was an acceptable situation. Since their world had been restricted to them for a long time they had found subtle ways to communicate. Rhona smiled to herself. She had been looking for love to fill the void in her life. Not finding a man in the academic world or in her church, here was one that figuratively fell into her lap. She liked his ruddy look, his soft-spoken voice, and the fact that they had a common bond in scientific training and practice. Most of all, she was attracted to his hands. The fingers seemed gentle and yet projected a strength of bearing. She had shunned placing herself in the category of a lonely and desperate woman but with her fortieth birthday looming on the horizon, it was becoming more difficult to resign to a life empty of romance and companionship.

Parker found her easy to talk with. They conversed nearly the entire flight time, and he was definitely attracted to her. It was natural to compare her to Myrna, and there were numerous apparent similarities. Beyond the daughters, Rhona had a keen sense of humor, a warm and easy smile, and her mannerism and graciousness protruded with genuineness. During extensive discussions about psychological theories, there was little doubt that this woman was very intelligent. He tried not to think beyond the moment but it was readily apparent that a dilemma was brewing. Especially was this in the offing when it was discovered that Rhona's parents were only a few miles from Clarisse.

As it worked out, Parker actually saw more of Rhona and Franny than he did of Clarisse over the holiday period. Clarisse was involved in a pressing real estate sale that depended on a zoning variance that she had trouble pursuing because of the holiday closing of county offices. So, while she ran around, Parker saw Rhona just about most of the days and all of the nights. Bountiful moments were shared and enjoyed.

Parker talked to Myrna a few times on the telephone. Undoubtedly because of the lawyer meetings and her family festivities she did not detect the slight hesitation in his voice. Of course, she and Gabby talked endlessly about Parker to family and friends, totally unaware that the seemingly cemented relationship was in danger of crumbling apart. In fact, it was the thought of Parker and his love that gave Myrna the wherewithal to weather the meeting with her lawyer. That meeting ushered in the lawyer's opinion as he had offered earlier that George was not really interested in custody but saw this as an opportunity to get out from under the support order. It was just an issue of how much he would push for it. He could demand a hearing, and that would put additional financial strain on him as well as on Myrna. They discussed the possibility of calling his bluff and offer him partial custody. Myrna thought that this was too risky. She would not part with Gabby for a moment. So, with this situation hanging over her head the holiday festivities were dulled for her. Gabby immersed herself in the Christmas spirit assured that her mother's love would protect her. The innocence of childhood is one of the most precious human features. It is doomed by its fragility in a world filled with forces, events and people intent on taking it away. Once it has fleeted it is gone forever.

> *The tragedy of life is not that it ends*
> *so soon, but that we wait so long to*
> *begin it.*
>
> W.M. Lewis

THIRTEEN

The campus at Blantyre University was a surreal setting, as most college campuses are when the mass of students is away. The winds carry the anguish of ghosts with no academic life to drown them out. All can have a special significance to those who sojourn along the pathways and who dare to tempt the ghosts in their travail. Yet, they have cries of their own, for they have given up something to be back early. Some hear and respect the voices of the winds and abide by the majesty of the mountains. Some even have the privilege of discovering secrets harbored deep within themselves.

Drake and Alexa met at the diner just beyond the rolling lawns, now covered by a layer of snow. With the wintry chill outside, they embraced and the warmth was comforting. A kiss followed naturally, and it was steeped with a meaning each appreciated. There was no need for words. Deep emotions require no vocal pronouncements. The fulfillment is no less real, no less impacting.

Neither one would be able to recall with any specific clarity the chain of events leading to their being in Alexa's bed for the night. It was the first sexual encounter for each of them, although that would not be an apt description of the coupling. It was more of an affirmation of their closeness. It was a celebration of their togetherness. It was greater than an emotional release and tantamount to the recognition of the realization that their individual worlds had been righted. Physical and emotional satisfaction had merged to produce a consolidated contentment.

No one else would notice, and no one else would care. This was their private victory.

Alexa was the first to speak, the moments of silence and pleasure written in their hearts. "Where have you been all of my life?" She stroked his cheek, warm and tender to her touch. She could not help but think it reflected his whole being.

"I guess I have always been here. All you had to do was to reach out and reel me in."

"To clutch you to the real me."

"It just took a glimpse of such reality to convince me that wonderful moments need not be analyzed. A simple beauty is to just accept happiness wherever and whenever it happens. The good doctor is so right when he says that our personalities are distinctively our own and we need to just accept the good things for what they are. Then, to learn from the bad things, adjust the frame of reference accordingly, and go on from there. A rather simple formula and yet so hard to grasp."

The next morning they did not notice the cold as they walked to the diner for breakfast. Arm was locked in arm, and heart was embraced by heart. The missing element in their lives had been supplied, proving the new math that it often takes two to make one. There was no reason to probe or question this love, or even to ponder its direction or duration. It consumed the here and now, and that was its magic. For two weak souls, the existence was its strength. They no longer needed Dr. Benson.

> *The greatest happiness of life is the conviction*
> *that we are loved – loved for ourselves,*
> *or rather, loved in spite of ourselves.*
> Victor Hugo

FOURTEEN

Magical moments were distant happenings for Rhona Kingsley. Even as a youngster experiences had tended to be painful. The elderly parents she was now visiting had given her a comfortable existence. They both worked at good jobs not realizing the lonely and detached times inflicted on their only child. She did not want Franny to be an only child either but until Parker came along there had been no one she had considered having a child with. Her first husband had been a weak and disoriented person, and after the divorce she drifted directionless and alone. Friendships and relationships were nonexistent. She avoided such opportunities even if they developed. Teaching became her salvation. It kept her thought processes intact and enabled her to anchor a meager life for herself and her daughter.

With Parker, the tilted world had regained its robust rightful posture. Taken completely by his gentle mannerism and caring gestures, it did not take long for Rhona to fall in love with him. Perhaps, it was even the first real love of her being. Added special significance revolved around his sincere attention to Franny. They talked and joked as if they had known each other for a long time. Franny was enthralled by him, and Rhona accepted that as another good sign.

Every moment they spent together was enchanting. She felt natural, and no inhibitions filtered into her speech or actions. Except for Franny's presence, she just would have asked him to share her bed at the motel. That is how sure she was that this man was the one she was waiting for. Her life had a marvelous new direction, a fresh meaning. Here was a wake up call to seize the happiness that had eluded her. This was her chance to live an optimistic approach that she had long preached for others. The note of optimism found in a poem by George Gordon was the theme she had used for her students in her classes at the college. The aptness filled her with new resolve.

> *I do believe*
> *though I found them not, that there may be*
> *words which are things, hopes which will not deceive*
> *and virtues which are merciful, nor weave*
> *snares for the failing: I would also deem*
> *that two, or one, are almost what they seem,*
> *that goodness is no name and happiness no dream.*

She also appreciated that Parker was her intellectual equal. The discussions were absorbing and stimulating. Their outlook and beliefs ran in tandem. She could not remember the last time she had a counterpart that required keen listening and keener thinking. Cultural compatibility threaded its way through likes and dislikes. Even the mutual love of classical music presented a special romantic backdrop to their togetherness.

With Franny around all of the time, they had to capture whatever private moments they could. It was not until the night before they were to depart back to Boston that they made love. Even that was hastened, and she had taken a room in a different motel just down the road. Franny was glued to the television in the regular room, and they escaped to the other room for an hour. As rushed as it was, the sweet and endearing touches and whispers did not disappoint. He brought her flesh to life, and she savored the sensations she only guessed she was capable of. His body was not strange to her. Brevity forced her to hasten her explorations. Yet, it was like an old friend. Comfort comes at times not with familiarity but with the desire to be familiar.

For Parker, it seemed as if it was a natural culmination of their being together. His strong feelings for this new woman in his life placated the knowledge that he was in some way disloyal to Myrna. A predicament loomed before him and it would have to be faced. Meanwhile, he held this tender and refreshing woman close to his heart, and his arms enfolded a significance he might later analyze but could not deny. Her tears of happiness fell upon his chest. Could a man love two women? From not loving to a point where he did love two, was his torment just beginning by loving too much and too many? This moment would end. Another moment would begin, and the moments might be arduous instead of ardent.

> *What you leave behind is not what is engraved in stone monuments, but what is woven into the lives of others.*
> Pericles

FIFTEEN

The odd aspect concerning feeling good about oneself is that it usually does not last long. There are too many forces, too many extant pressures tugging at the unity of thought and emotion. Sheila Levine was not in the cramped tenement apartment long before the nagging and intractability of her parents cracked her resolve. She had braced herself for it hoping to be fortified long enough to leave for the visit to her aunt, but it did put a damper on the respite from her studies. She had immersed herself in the books once Roger exited from her life. At least she did not have to contend with that additional burden and complication to her well-being. Actually, she was looking forward to another session with Dr. Benson. It had been beneficial telling someone her thoughts and feelings and not being judged about them.

She was well aware that this was a crucial juncture in her life. It was evident that she had to proceed on her own. The determination to succeed would undoubtedly carry her through. But what might be the cost? To shun family and friends, as well as to avoid love so that principles need not be compromised, was not an especially appealing course of action. Yet, as long as she had someone to talk to, someone to bolster any sagging weaknesses, she would be fine. Part of her new found strength was that she knew she could talk herself in or out of any conflict.

Still, hovering above all this was a kind of loneliness, a loneliness that particularly haunted her at awkward moments. A disenchantment and disassociation from her family and from her religious background left her thirsting for emotional fulfillment.

85

It would be difficult to describe to Dr. Benson since she was not sure she could even delineate it for herself. Because of that strict religious upbringing, demonstrative affection in the household was rare. Urges for displays of affection had been stifled, and it was problematic how she might react now. Roger's concept of a relationship had been sexual in nature, and she had never felt any desire to hold his hand, caress his arm, or kiss him on her own initiative. If she waited for sex until after marriage, there would necessarily be affection coupled with it. It would be an integral part. This may not be a lawyer's logic but it made sense to her.

Even a visit to Aunt Sarah proved unfulfilling. She just did not have the enthusiasm to bridge the generation gap, even though she loved that aunt dearly as she was truly the only one in her family that she felt a closeness to. So, she returned to Blantyre early, explaining that extra time was needed to complete numerous term papers. Solitude can be a kindly companion. The peaceful campus and long bracing walks in the frigid air filled her with emotional and physical vigor. On just one of these walks, and not expecting to see another soul since the campus was deserted, a young man approached her from the opposite direction. A muffler hid most of his face, and a wool cap was pulled down to his eyes. He pulled down the muffler to reveal a smile, and she smiled slightly in return. After passing each other, he turned around, caught up with her, and said in a pleasant voice, "You're Levine, aren't you?"

She looked closely at the part of the youthful face that she could see. "Yes, but I am not sure who you are."

"I am not sure who I am at times either." He matched her long strides. "I am in your Foreign Policy class. I am quiet compared to your sharp comments to the professor. I think of things to say, but you have already beat me to it."

"Oh. I get overwound at times when things just don't seem right to me."

"Don't get me wrong. It is not a bad thing to air your challenges. You make up for those as I am, strong in mind and conviction but meek in production."

"Easily rectified if you just let yourself loose from the shackles of reservedness."

"Uncomplicated for you, but a tough barrier for me. Aren't you in the least bit curious to know who I am?"

"Curiosity is for children. If you want me to know your name don't let shyness hinder you."

"Carl."

"So, Carl, why aren't you home or chasing hotties on a Florida beach?"

"Home was a negative environment, and hotties are not my thing."

"They're every man's thing. Just let your testosterone take over."

"Do you always give advice to people you do not know?"

"Or do not care to know." She paused and turned to him. "Sorry, that was not a kind remark."

They resumed walking. "That's alright. I chalk it up to you being honest. I already know from class that you speak your mind."

"If I can do it, so can you."

"I'm trying right now. Why are you back here early?"

"A negative home environment."

"I seem to have heard that before. I cannot keep calling you Levine. What is your first name?"

"If I told you that it would be a form of encouragement that perhaps I wanted to be your friend. I don't want any male friends."

"That's rather limiting, don't you think?"

"It's the testosterone thing again."

"Wow. Maybe I had you all wrong. Maybe you do not speak from an open mind but are as opinionated as those that you challenge."

"Maybe. Why should you care?"

"I might if I wanted to be your friend. Since that does not seem to be in the cards, I just want to make sure you see more to me than a guy who wants to deflower you."

"Is there more to see?"

"I like to think so."

She kept her eyes riveted straight in front of her, torn between a challenge and an inner desire to regain her solitude. "Convince me then."

"Convince me that you want to be convinced."

"You're a hard nose. I can tell that about you."

"Probably just your type."

"Is that what you think of me?"

Carl drew quiet for a moment. "Sounds like you are convinced already. You are asking me my opinion of you."

"There is more to people than tricks, you know."

He tried to show a serious look on his face. "I do know that. It is difficult to learn but once you do it stays with you."

"Everything you learn should stay with you."

"I am learning to like you, in spite of yourself. Will you stay with me?"

She looked at him sternly, "Stay like in sleep with you?"

"No. Not that. Stay with me so we can have dinner together."

"You had better know right away that I am a prude."

"I love prunes."

She couldn't help herself and smiled broadly. "I said prude, not prune."

"There will come a day when you are older when you may learn to appreciate prunes."

"That would be the pits."

Carl chuckled. They walked along in silence for a few minutes. He was quite taken by this young woman. He thought she was the prettiest girl he had ever seen, and he admired her in class as she openly challenged what he secretly questioned. He liked that spirit.

Now that it had taken hold of her attention, Sheila was glad this young man diverted her from the preoccupation with herself. "Alright," she spoke softly, "I will have dinner with you. Just know that I do not do sex and I don't do prunes."

"Fine. I don't do sex with anyone who does not do sex. I might, however, in a wild moment have a prune. That's as wild as I get."

She smiled as she walked closer to his side. "My name is Sheila."

We are each of us angels with only one wing,
and we can only fly by embracing one another.

Lucretius

SIXTEEN

Later that night as Carl Bishop lay in his dorm bed, he was too keyed up to sleep. The dorm was eerily quiet since he was one of a handful of students returning before the resumption of classes. His reason for an early return was much more complicated than just a description of a negative home environment that he had tossed out to Sheila. He was also hoping to see Dr. Benson. He had heard such wonderful things about the man, and even if it was unlikely Carl hoped that the Doctor was around during the holiday break. He did not know that Sheila was his patient, but that would only have solidified his urgency to get help.

Of course, he was not the only child coming from a broken home. His home, however, had not been a normal one to begin with. His parents had married in the face of strong opposition from families and friends. Inter-denominational marriages were not as uncommon as they had been in the past, and generally more accepted. Both families had a strong bias and there just was no way to reconcile disbeliefs and misconceptions. Ostracized and verbally castigated they clung to one another, and actually were driven further into action than they might have been if left alone. Besides the religion factor, his parents had a number of other issues and if not pressured they might very well have discovered that they were not right for one another. To show up the world, they eloped

The marriage did not stop the opposition or calm their differences, accentuated upon the birth of Carl. Even having a child did not bring any of the family members closer or forgiving. At what age Carl became aware of the lack of tranquility was immaterial because the friction had already taken its toll. He was antagonistic to playmates, rebellious to authority, and rarely smiled. His growing years were not happy times, and it did not get any better when he lived with his mother after the divorce. His mother never was welcomed back into the family, and she struggled to cope emotionally on many fronts. She had nothing to do with her ex-husband, and in turn Carl's father neglected him.

In spite of this tortured childhood, Carl's turnaround occurred in high school. Studies began to absorb his interest, and he read voraciously. A subjugated intelligence emerged, and he became an academic champion. It was a silent accomplishment as his participation in the classes was severely limited. Examinations were the easy pathway for him. He graduated as the valedictorian of his class and received an academic scholarship to Blantyre. He had few friends as his quietness repulsed his lively counterparts. Even the brief speech he made at the graduation ceremony was coolly received, and he barely believed for himself the advice he gave to the others that life beckoned and should be fully followed.

There had been only one romantic encounter, and it was not at school. There he silently longed for several females from afar only. He was drawn to the quiet ones, and he romanticized them as figures in books. One summer he worked as a file clerk at an insurance company. One of the young women in the typing pool kept smiling at him, and they started having lunch together in the lunchroom. Her name was Harper, and she had long, shiny black hair, dark eyes and a slim figure. She was several years older than him. One time they found themselves alone behind a row of file cabinets. She pulled him towards her and kissed him deeply. She took his hand and placed it on her breast. He could feel its softness beneath her blouse. She started sending him little notes professing a love for him. Just when he felt an aggressive force emerging, he discovered she was married. That scared him, and at the end of the summer he politely said goodbye to her. The glisten in her eyes was evident, and it was then and there that he vowed that because his life had been filled with hurt and disappointment he would never intentionally hurt another human being.

That Sheila looked a bit like Harper led him to a gradual worship of her. He stared at her in class. He had not dated since being at Blantyre, and he had kept a straight A average to perpetuate the scholarship. Each time that Sheila spoke out, Carl's interest and desire were sparked. When he came across her on the path of the campus, he surprised himself that he could think and speak. Up close she was most alluring. Beauty and brains in one package. How could he resist that?

He had returned to the campus early because being with his mother had become unbearable. She inwardly blamed him for the downturn in her life. Her bitterness grew and was overwhelming her. Her drinking became an easy outlet, and she was a pitiful and despotic figure when drunk. The smell of alcohol revolted him. The stench of a home not really a home seared his very core.

Now, a senior, and still young, he had a debilitating feeling that he was still squandering his youth. Missed or bungled opportunities, and experiences not built upon. At the age of twenty-one he had a dismal impression that life had left him far behind. Sheila did not have to worry about having sex with him. After all, he would not even know how to begin to undertake such a mysterious endeavor. Once, he had gone over to Sue Lynn's house to tutor her in algebra. Her parents were out and she was wearing satin lounging pajamas. He could see her unrestrained breasts jiggle under the shiny fabric as she walked. She saw him staring at them. "Do you want to see them?" His lips were dry and the palms of his hands sweaty. "They are quite a handful. I'll show them to you if you pass the answers to me for the next test." In hindsight, he should have agreed just to see what would have happened. He could have made a hundred excuses later on for not complying with cheating. For all he knew, she did not give a hoot about algebra but just wanted to have sex with him. Why else would she have dressed like that? Anyway, he had said sternly that he could not pass answers to her. They went on with the tutoring, and his eyes rarely left her chest. He could only speculate what might have happened. His fear had ushered in hesitation. That can be a seed for regret. He had learned that all too well.

He thought he had handled himself very well with Sheila. At dinner, there was much to talk about and the conversation came easily. They had much in common. Both had academic scholarships, both were political science majors, and both were tentative in social situations. She planned to go to law school while he wanted to teach at the college level for which he would undoubtedly have to go for Master's and Doctoral degrees. Neither wanted to ever go home again.

They had made a date for the following evening to have dinner together at the diner since the cafeteria would not reopen until after the new year arrived. Neither had a car but it was not a far walk to the edge of the campus where the diner was located. Even a sharp cold wind and snow flurries did not daunt their undertaking. Symbolically, it merely drew them closer together, fighting the outside elements.

The homemade vegetable soup was most satisfying. They slurped it loudly in the nearly deserted place. Each had made a discovery in themselves and in each other, even if it had yet to be fully defined.

The conversation was jovial and light through the meal. It turned serious as they ate apple pie with their coffee. Each described in detail the home environment which led to an early return. She did not have to but she told him about seeing Dr. Benson and that she had felt so much better when he had assured her that she did not have to succumb to sexual pressures. Carl confided in her that he was back early in part to also see the good doctor to discuss his social stultification. Sheila showed some surprise as she did not think he was socially inept.

She looked at him intently. "You say you come from a mixed marriage. What religions?"

He studied that pretty and earnest face before responding. "My mother is Jewish and my father is Catholic."

"Wow. Quite a combination, even in this day and age. My parents are strict Jews."

"I was raised as an agnostic. Frankly, I do not believe in a God. From my parent's poor example and experience, I am not sure I believe in love either."

She glanced off into the darkness through the window. It had started snowing heavily, and she likened her being to a snowflake cascading aimlessly down from a dark sky. "My jewishness is merely a convenient label. I suppose it gave me a sense of belonging as I grew up. Now, I am not sure what I believe in other than in myself. I want to be the finest lawyer I can be and the best person. Some would say those goals are incompatible. I don't accept that. I will make it work. I will make it happen."

"I am sure you will."

"I am confident that you will also make a fine professor. We'll be graduating together, and dreams do not stop there."

"Maybe that is where they actually begin."

"That is a wonderful thought."
"We can certainly spend some time together until then."
"I would like that. I feel close to you."
"Me too."

> *Love is not what you are, but what you*
> *may become.*

Miguel de Cervantes Saavedra

SEVENTEEN

The drive back seemed especially long. It was comforting for Myrna seeing Gabby curled up on the back seat reading or doing puzzles. The excitement of seeing Parker again was building up. She needed to feel his comforting arms around her. She needed to know that in this cruel, cold and uncertain world a place of refuge existed. At least she was distancing herself from the possibility of the legal challenge to her custody of Gabby.

Arriving at the house, it was disappointing to get the telephone message from Parker that he would not be back until the following day and would have to go directly to the office since it was the first day of classes after the holiday break. For an instant the hint of a hurt emerged. Was he not as anxious to be with her as she was for him? Quickly dismissing the negative thought, she reveled in being sure of him. He had become the anchor to keep her steadily in place.

Gabby hurried upstairs to sort out all of her Christmas presents. She was hoping the doc would be here, but the thought passed as she immersed herself in prioritizing the bounty. She was excited about returning to school, and a couple of special items would be shown to her friends. One was the charm bracelet the doc gave her before they left. It made her feel grown up. She had never heard of charm bracelets, and her mother's explanation of its lasting significance was still fresh in her mind. She would also make sure she had it on when the doc came over.

Parker and Rhona clenched hands tightly as the plane landed in Boston. Snow flurries filled the dark sky even though it was barely 10:00 A.M. Parker knew he would continue his self-discussion during the two-hour drive to Blantyre. Rhona had only a twenty-minute trip but was reluctant to undo her embrace of Parker as they parted to go their separate ways. He knew he should have told her about Myrna. It was either the coward or the dreamer in him that did not want to intrude on the captivation. What would he counsel one of his patients about facing the inevitable? Do it now or put it off for as long as possible?

Rhona and Franny were highly animated during the short drive to the apartment near the college. It had turned out to be a wonderful Christmas after all. The depressing visit with her dying parents, the only relatives she had, was way offset by the new man in her life. Franny was happy to see her mother so relaxed and enjoying even the small moments they spent together. It bode well. She had been worried about her mother. It seemed as if she never had any fun.

Arlene glared at Parker as he entered the reception area. "You're morning appointments are still waiting. There'll be more coming through the door any time now."

"Please see if you can reschedule the afternoon appointments. It will take me the rest of the day to see the folks that are already here."

Sitting behind his desk he took a deep breath. Sorting out his own dilemma would have to wait. He was a professional and these students needed him. He picked up the telephone and asked Arlene to send in the first appointment.

Somehow Gloria Hastings had not minded waiting the three hours to see Dr. Benson, and the thought that she was missing classes did not bother her as if that mattered at all anymore. She had been in a haze since Christmas day, and everything appeared unreal.

Sitting before the doctor, she could not bring herself to look him in the eyes. She had to subdue a tendency to get up and run away and never stop running.

Parker sensed a troubled woman before him, and he was going to castigate her for not filling out the pre-interview form other than with her name when he thought better of it. "I apologize for being late. It was kind of you to wait this long, Gloria. May I call you Gloria?"

She nodded, and Parker noted her slumping shoulders and a slight quiver at the corner of her mouth. The red hair was barely combed and there was no make up on the slim face.

"Would you like a glass of water?"

Again she nodded. He fetched it and after handing it to her he sat on the corner of the desk close to her. "I am here for you to talk with. But, we don't have to talk just yet. Try to relax. When you feel comfortable you can say as little or as much as you want. I have not seen you before so I expect something has happened recently that has upset you. We can approach that when you are ready, whether it be today or at a later visit if that works better for you."

She finally looked at him, and through tightly clenched lips the voice was quivering. "I best tell you now. My courage to speak about it may never come again. I won't be here to tell you later." She took a sip of the water, and the glass slipped through her fingers and shattered on the linoleum floor. "Sorry," she uttered and bent to pick up the broken pieces.

He placed his hand on her arm stopping her. He gently coaxed her back to a sitting position. Her comments certainly alerted him to trouble. "That can wait until later."

Gloria sat back in the chair and crossed her jean-clad legs. It was then that he noticed she had two different styled loafers on her feet. Both were black but one was plain and the other had tassels. "Would you like another glass of water?"

She shook her head. "Please be patient with me."

"I can be no other way. I am trained to be that way, although I like to think it is my natural inclination anyway. If I cannot be that way in the face of the problems of those who come to see me, I would have no right to be here."

He was not sure if she heard him, or if she did whether the significance of the words registered in her frame of reference. She began speaking, the voice stronger than it had been. "I don't really know how to begin. It is painful to talk about, especially since it is so much more than just my pain."

Parker moved back to his chair, sensing that not being too close might give an impetus for her to open up more. During her hesitation she may have accepted the notion that it might be right to speak about her plight, particularly to a stranger. After all, she was here because she wanted to be.

She cleared her throat and continued. "My parents are now in their late sixties. My mother had me when she was forty-nine. It surprised and delighted her, and they kept calling me the miracle baby. What added to the special event was that I was a girl, and there are two older brothers. It went downhill from there."

Again, another hesitation, and the tears welled up in her eyes. "My brother, Bobby, was killed in a terrible car crash when he was sixteen. The family was crushed. My other brother, Frank, now thirty-seven, lived by himself in an apartment a few miles from our house. It was strange that he did not show up on Christmas morning. We called several times. My father went over there." Another gap in the narration, then tears flowing even more. "He found him dead. He died of a drug overdose. Two children gone, and my parents and I are completely devastated. Above and beyond that, they are now convinced that I am also fated to meet a terrible and untimely death. They want me close by, and allowed me only to return here to pack up my things and withdraw from the school. My father is coming for me tomorrow to take me home."

Parker was saddened by this story, and his heart reached out for a young person having to bear such sorrow. He pulled a tissue from the box on the desk and handed it to her. "Gloria, I know it is painful to live through this, and it may be one of the few situations where it is not much help to talk about it. Do you share your parent's view on fate?"

She shook her head, the tears still flowing. "I don't want to believe it. My father is convinced that the family is jinxed, like the Kennedy's."

"If I believed in fate than I would not be able to guide my patients. Things would be preordained and beyond my advice. Your family tragedy, as the turn of events with families such as the Kennedy's, is merely a horrific flow of circumstances. Threads of belief can often be found between cruel occurrences but that does not mean they are interrelated. If you believe that, in time you will be able to make your parents see that you need to be you and they need to release any seemingly protective actions. The latest shock is still too fresh for them to focus rationally. Give it and them time to sort it all out. Being with them so they feel they are protecting you may be just the comfort they need right now. It may be solace for you as well. You can grieve together. You will be free from academic pressures. I will always be available if you need to talk. While only full time students are entitled without cost to be my patients, I can arrange an exception for you. What I have said is based on a most caring intent. Please take it in that spirit. I only hope it makes some sense and will assist you in taking each day as it comes along. After all, that is just about what any of us can do in this world. Take one day at a time."

She dabbed her eyes as the tear fountain stopped gushing.

"Actually, what you have said just echoes what I have been thinking and apprehensive to accept. I guess more than anything I am afraid. I am not afraid that I might have an accident but afraid that nothing in my life will approach normalcy ever again. I loved my brothers and they are gone. I love my parents and know they will never fully heal from this latest blow to their world. In a way, I have lost them too."

Parker wished he could ease her burden. "Events have catapulted you to where you may have to be the strongest force in your family. Young people should not have the carefree days of youth cut short, but there are demanding times that call for such courage. I am sure you are up to it. Be sure of that yourself. You can and will do what you have to do. Believe it. Believe in yourself."

After Gloria left, Parker picked up the broken pieces of glass. Lives can be shattered as well. The secret is not to dwell on the broken pieces but to try and mend what can be saved. Somehow he felt that Gloria would do that. If only young people had the same faith in themselves as he had in them.

> *Wisdom is ofttimes nearer when we*
> *stoop than when we soar.*
> William Wordsworth

EIGHTEEN

There was a tentativeness in the embrace and the slightest hesitation in his kiss. Myrna had always been ultra perceptive as to human emotions and very sensitive to body signs. Just as she knew from the first meeting that Parker was interested in her, she now sensed a barrier to his will and outpouring. If he said nothing about it, after Gabby went to bed she would raise the matter. After all, she wanted no more clouds in her life.

Parker was certainly confused. Back with Myrna and Gabby he felt at ease and appreciated the loving overtures both extended to him. It warmed his heart to see Gabby make a continuous point of displaying the charm bracelet he had given her. There was one apparent conclusion. He was in love with two women, endeared to two families. How could he possibly explain it to them when he could not decipher it himself?

The tact Myrna was going to take came to her as she was tucking Gabby into bed. Gabby was exhausted and it would not take her long to fall asleep.

She came downstairs and sat next to Parker on the sofa. She looked deeply into his eyes. "When Gabby was younger, she went through a period being fascinated by science fiction. The notion took hold that her real mother had been abducted by aliens and had been replaced by one of their own disguised as me. She would put her ear to my chest to listen for a heart beat. She would ask me all sorts of questions to make sure I was the real me. She was convinced only her real mother would know the proper answers. Then she would, as the final test, make me hug her as only I can do. I have an inkling that you have been replaced by an alien. Hold me and kiss me to assure me you are who you claim to be."

Parker held her in a tight embrace and kissed her tenderly. "Convinced?"

"Almost. Kiss me again."

He obliged. "Need more proof?"

"I guess not but I sense something is wrong."

"One of the many qualities I love about you is your perceptiveness. I was not going to explain anything to you until I sorted it out in my own mind. But, since you sense my quandary, I want to be truthful to you in all regards. I need to tell you what happened on my trip to Florida."

Parker recited the turn of events as best as he was able without any embellishments. He knew it would be hurtful and yet he knew that the pain would be greater if he held back on something that might emerge later.

As much as she fought it, Myrna could not prevent the tears swelling in her eyes. She had thought that one of the problems of Parker's student clients had gotten hold of him and was bothering him. This was far worse, and a direct threat to her life and as a woman.

Myrna knew he was waiting for her response. It was spontaneous. "If I said this was not painful I would be lying. I am just a plain and simple country girl. I cannot compete with this kind of sophisticated woman, especially one who can talk psychology with you until the cows come home. All I know is that Gabby and I love you. I do not take that love lightly. I am not going to force you to choose or make any decisions now. I suppose when you are ready, that will come of its own. What I do know is that I am not going to give up on you or us. I will fight for you with everything I can be. If that is not enough, then I suppose we are not meant to be. I have lost and gained much in my life. I won't lose you, and I am confident about that. My love for you is special and will remain that way. You will realize it. Of that I am sure. Forgive me for rambling but it is my way of venting my frustration. I have no control over this situation. You do."

He embraced her again. "What you said was beautiful. It was so honest, so you. You and Gabby are precious to me. I love you dearly. In the 60s a very controversial novel was published, entitled *The Rebellion of Yale Marratt*. It is about a young man who falls in love with two women, marries them both, and the women accept each other and they live as a threesome. He then starts a movement to legitimize bigamy. I read the book back then because of its attack on society's staid mores and all the psychological overtones. At the time, I thought the premise was unrealistic. How could a person love two people that way? I may have been quite wrong about that."

She took his silence as a cue to speak. "You might be able to share your love with two women. I cannot accept another woman encroaching on the love I feel for you. As selfish as I am, I will not share you. As I said, I will not force you to choose between us but in the final analysis it probably will come to that." It struck her by using the term *final analysis* she was perhaps replicating a psychological nuance, or at least what seemed to be that. If this were not so serious she could be smug about her description. Her stomach churned, and she felt clammy. Just as she was starting to build a protective edifice, between the effort to take Gabby from her and Parker's hesitation, her walls were crumbling around her. Somehow, she would keep herself together. She knew she had to do that. If not for herself, it had to be done for Gabby so her world would be fortified.

Under these same circumstances, another woman might have denied him her sexual favors. For her, that would be cutting her nose off to spite her face. She needed him and wanted him to realize that as well as knowing that he needed her. The lovemaking was warm and gentle, and distracted thoughts did not detract from the robust pleasure.

Powerful forces were working on Parker. Many of his basic qualities were being tested. There was no way he could have prepared for such an inner conflict. However it might conclude, he was certain he would find out just what kind of person he is.

> *A man can fail many times, but he isn't a failure*
> *until he begins to blame somebody else.*
> John Burroughs

NINETEEN

Since beginning his duties at Blantyre, Parker had only students as patients. So, on the next day it came as a bit of a surprise when Arlene told him that John Maxwell, Professor of American History, wanted to see him professionally as soon as possible. The schedule was already overburdened and Arlene was instructed to try and squeeze the Professor in. Arlene, as a magician in her secretarial ways, was able to accomplish this and to notify the Professor of the appointment.

Personal problems are a major source of discontent, and even if the problem is not an unusual one it still can take a debilitating toll on the individual. Being close to the situation often clouds perception of both the details and the context surrounding the issue. Even if a viable solution may become apparent, the capacity to execute it may be arduous. As an intellect, Professor Maxwell had wrestled with finding a solution on his own. The possibilities were as bad as the problem. He was also aware that his own weaknesses were intensified by the problem and would further handicap any resolution. He hoped that all of the good things that he had heard about Parker would rescue him from a growing torment. His training in history and the concentration of looking backwards in time seemed far removed from a science that crossed all time thresholds.

Parker knew the Professor by sight and reputation. He reminded him of a television actor picked because of his professorial look. A thick head of hair with graying temples and horn-rimmed glasses added to the illusion of being distinguished. A deep and resonant voice rounded out the stature. He was probably in his forties, Parker would guess. "Thank you for seeing me on such short notice. A teacher can learn from his students, and I have heard a number of them refer to you as a life saver."

"Probably an elaboration just for a helping hand or word. Reputations can be fragile commodities. A hero one day, a fool the next."

"As well I know that. In this day and age it is most difficult to maintain being an academic icon. The gap between expectations and reality is a dangerous abyss."

"How can I help the icon?"

Professor Maxwell leaned back in the chair. The shoulders slumped a bit, and his lips appeared dry and parched. "I have been a teacher here for nearly fifteen years. I can think of no better life. I need to avoid jeopardizing that." He paused for a few seconds, taking off his glasses and then placing them firmly back on his head. "I suppose I should preface this by saying that I have a family that I love dearly, and I do not want to put that at risk. Over the years, I have had my share of cunning coeds each vying for a good grade in exchange for some favor. There has been no problem rebuking such advances. Now, however, through my own devices and imagination, I have fallen under the spell of one of my students. She has not approached me in any way. Yet, she radiates such an aura of innocence and beauty that I am distracted at the sake of everything else. She is in my thoughts constantly. I have made no overtures towards her, and I dare not, but it is at the point that she haunts my very being. I am not sure how much longer I can keep any semblance of control over myself. I never realized that temptation could be so powerful. So, as embarrassing as it may be, that is my problem. Is there any way that you can help me?"

This is a tough call, Parker thought to himself. He could try to project himself into the Professor's position and guess how he might handle such a quandary. But, it might be best if he approached this as he does with the problems posed by the students. "As I tell each student when he or she brings in an issue for resolution, I really cannot solve the problem for them. We can discuss options or just venting feelings can often be beneficial. The bottom line is that only the person with the difficulty can and should find whatever answer fits. I have been confronted by similar temptations by some of my female patients. There is no denying that a young female has a special allure. One in particular literally throws herself at me. She is gorgeous, and I am only human. Yet, I realize that her feelings and expressions are just masking a different sort of conflict. By fixing on me, she avoids and evades her deep-seeded personal dilemma. Perhaps, there is a similar scenario with you. The student may represent a convenient fixation for you to suffer over in place of another aspect of your life. Is your relationship with your wife satisfactory?"

Professor Maxwell shuddered slightly, a brow raised nearly noticeable. "After many years, a marriage becomes comfortable. That is satisfying in its own way. My wife is a wonderful person, admired by all. She has many friends and activities, and I do feel at times that I am on the periphery of her existence. Common interests have dwindled. Affection is less demonstrative."

"Do you think it is possible that you have transferred to this young woman a desire to put more excitement into your own marriage?"

"Possible, I suppose. But why wouldn't I have succumb to the easier presented opportunities?"

"Maybe because the battle with your conscience is greatest when the objective is unattainable, or at least appears that way."

"I am not sure any pang of conscience can subdue the pull

of will towards her."

"Maybe not. But, if you step back in your own mind and analyze the situation anew with this added ingredient, there might be a different view of the situation. Then if you contemplate it long and hard enough, maybe you can channel the impulse in an entirely different direction. Undertake a project with this passion you possess, like writing a book. I tend to think of human emotions as liquid and fluid in shape and density so that their direction can be altered rather than as a solid which is intractable. Try projecting the symbol of the young lady upon your wife and play out a fantasy with her. Does this make any sense?"

The Professor looked glum but there was no longer a deep furrow in his brow. "Fodder for thought for sure. Thank you for seeing me. It does help to express one's feelings. I can see why the students think so highly of you. I join their ranks and applaud you."

> *People spend a lifetime searching for happiness,*
> *looking for peace. They chase idle dreams,*
> *addictions, religions, even other people, hoping*
> *to fill the emptiness that plagues them.*
> *The irony is the only place they ever*
> *needed to search was within.*
> Ramona L. Anderson

TWENTY

As the arrival time drew near, the excitement grew to near fever pitch. Rhona and Franny stared out of the apartment window looking anxiously for Parker's car to pull up to the building. Rhona was in an extreme state of rapture. Dwelling on the loving thoughts of Parker and their brief time together, there was no denying her love for him. He represented all that she ever had desired. With terminal parents, no relatives and no really close friends, this brightness in her dark world was long overdue. Even Franny sensed the dynamic change in her mother's disposition. Seeing her mother upbeat and smiling so easily was truly wonderful for her as it would be for any child bound so close to a mother. The frequent laughing was the best part. That was contagious. There was a place in her own heart for this man that had transformed her mother into such a happy person. From such warm beginnings dreams are created and lived.

The weekend proved to be a warm and relaxing time for all. Franny accepted her mother's statement that Parker would be sharing her bed, and she did not think twice about it. That bed sharing was the crowning touch for Parker and Rhona. Tender touches led to gentle moments of pleasure. A warm contentment enveloped them and seemingly conveyed to them that deep feelings are the bedrock of a special relationship.

The time went by all too quickly. Late on Sunday, Parker started his trip back to Blantyre. He had every intention of telling Rhona about Myrna but probably as an act of cowardice he rationalized that such a revelation would disturb the pleasant mood.

Rhona cried after he left, and it was not an easy task to explain to Franny that they were tears of happiness. She had always been afraid to ask too much from life. Now, life was giving her more than she had dared to hope for. As she explained to her students, emotion is what leads one to living and sustains a will to live.

Myrna was tempted to ask him how the weekend went. The thought was dismissed. It was better to leave things alone at this point. She was still confident that with time and some gentle and subtle revelations Parker would come to realize that true love, true family bonding was here with her and Gabby. That confidence left her calmer, so that when Parker arrived for dinner that Monday evening she just reveled in the enjoyment of his company. In her bed, she let her hands travel the course over his body conveying the pathway he should follow.

Confidence could be found elsewhere on the Blantyre campus. Sheila and Carl had been seeing a great deal of each other. They shared a mutual respect that grew to a confidence in their togetherness. The discussion of their relationship took an interesting turn as they became aware that there had been much touching and hugging. Such actions had been scant in their lives, and it was as if they were making up for lost time and lessons. These amorous undertakings added great value to their emotional and intellectual intertwinement. The first kiss, complete with a first exhibition of passion, sealed a pact between them. Despite growing sexual urges, Carl did not want to press Sheila to forego her avowed chastity. He knew that it meant more for her than just a refrain from sex. It was a principle that she needed to keep secure as a part of the totality of her integrity. Sharing the earnest desire to be close friends was ultimately satisfying. The surprising part was that it was an effortless journey. Sheila, for her part, was in love and it was that love that would dictate her behavior and not her mores. She wondered what it would be like if she let Carl make love to her. The concept no longer frightened her. It no longer seemed alien. The introduction of a person or an event can alter the scheme of a person's beliefs and endeavors. That sure is difficult to believe until experienced first-hand. Time would write that story.

Alexa and Drake had become inseparable, day and night. A desire to catch up on all that had been missing in their lives added deep passion to their actions, feelings and thoughts. Having each other, it was easy to distance themselves from any harsh intruding reality. Adopting such a formula for living, they were in control. Neither dared to face the future while so consumed by the present.

Parker needed more time to himself to sort out his vagabond ways. The weeks went by and he was no closer to any resolution of his predicament. He spent the entire between semester's break with Rhona and Franny, and his practice seemed distant to the memorable moments he accrued. Occasionally, a flash of professional curiosity would touch his mind as he wondered how the students and the Professor were meeting their trials. Yet, this appeared separate from his realm of involvement of the moment. Everything else melded together. When alone, he was the captain of his life's ship. When he was with Rhona or Myrna, the vessel floundered on an open, endless sea. He could not see the iceberg that lay ahead.

> *Don't go through life,*
> *grow through life.*
>   Eric Butterworth

TWENTY-ONE

When the telephone rings in the middle of the night, the chances are that it is not good news. Parker was jarred from an already restless sleep. He tried to clear his head as he reached for the receiver.

Rhona's voice was agitated. "Sweetheart, I need you. I am so sorry to disturb you, but I have no one else to turn to. They called me from the nursing home. Both of my parents are failing rapidly, almost in unison. Their time is very short. I have booked a flight first thing in the morning. I do not think Franny should go with me. She doesn't need this. I hate to ask. Can you come over right away and stay with her until I get back? It shouldn't be more than a couple of days."

"Of course. I will leave as soon as I can. I should be there by 6:00."

Her voice calmed a bit. "I just knew I could count on you. I love you so. I will make it up to you, I promise."

"There is nothing to make up for. I know you would be here if I needed you."

"Yes, I would, and gladly. See you soon my dearest man."

He actually arrived before the predicted time. He drove her to the airport. Franny, awakened before her usual arousal time was groggy and dozed in the back seat both to and from the airport. Rhona's fervent kiss was fresh on his lips as they arrived back at the apartment.

Rhona arrived at St. Augustine during a fierce wind and a driving rain. As soon as she landed she called the nursing home and was told that her parents were still barely hanging on. She rented a car, and the weather was no better as she drove out of the car rental lot. The route was not totally unfamiliar but the driving conditions did not prompt an easy trip. As the rain lashed against the windshield the wipers strained to keep vision clear. In fact, she did not see the pickup truck that went through a stop sign to her left, smashing forcefully into the car. When the police and ambulance arrived, it was determined that she had died immediately upon impact. The irony of it all was that her parents died four minutes apart before she even left the airport.

It was later in the day by the time that the police called the number in Rhona's wallet. All he could do was to slump down in a chair in total disbelief. Franny was not yet back from school, and that gave him a short period to try and accept the tragedy and adjust to how he might handle it with the youngster. Neither the acceptance nor the adjustment was complete. Sudden and dire circumstances often dictate an unplanned behavior.

Parker could figure no way to tell Franny except to explain as he was told what had happened. She did not take it well as he had feared. She cried long into the night, and eventually cried herself to sleep. It was only then that his tears flowed. Rhona's image hung over him like a thick cloud. He could scarcely believe that he would no longer gaze upon that serene and lovely face, never feel the warmth generated by her smile, and never again hug and kiss that lovely person close to his heart.

He reached out to the only voice that might comfort him. Myrna was shocked by the news and a genuine sympathy was offered. The tentacles of tragedy can touch many and alter their lives. Leaning on one another for support may lessen the overall debilitation.

He fell into an exhausting sleep in a chair and snapped

awake before sunrise. The obvious and demanding moment was that Franny had no one but him. He would contact a lawyer first thing to see about obtaining Franny's father's consent to Parker adopting her. He would also need legal guidance in tending to complete Rhona's affairs. A search of her desk revealed no will. The letter she left for him appointing him as Franny's guardian while she was away and giving him complete power to pursue any medical or other action for her well being should help facilitate any adoption. Franny also expressed her wish that he be with her.

After a few days, he knew he had to get back to Blantyre. Arlene could no longer stay the flood of appointments, and the Dean, while understanding, could no longer excuse any further absence. He left all of the procedures up to the attorney he had hired. They loaded Franny's meager furniture into a U-Haul and headed to Blantyre. Fortunately, he had two bedrooms in the town house, and he could just clear out the things he had in the second bedroom as a home office and set it up for her. Space was the least of the worry.

They hardly talked during the trip. Each was lost in the fog that shrouded them by the devastating development in their lives. The eventual intertwining of their lives had been accelerated. Franny was particularly solaced knowing that her mother was so happy before she died, that happiness all due to this kindly man who had assured her she would not be abandoned. Her mother loved him, and that love was transferred to her. This is what her mother would have wanted, of this she was sure. There would always be a hole in her heart. Yet, her mother had always emphasized that they needed to be resilient no matter what faced them.

They unloaded and in no time Franny had her own room set up. A trip to the grocery stocked the refrigerator and the kitchen cabinets. Parker was not used to cooking or caring for a youngster but Franny apparently was not fussy about food or pitching in to help with chores. Rhona had been an excellent parent and example.

Myrna was in a quandary. Her heart reached out to this little girl, especially since she was now part of Parker's world. Yet, it was the little child of a woman Parker apparently loved more than he cared about her. At least she did not have to worry about George's attempt to take Gabby away. That situation had been resolved when she agreed to forego any further support payments. So, she was able to generate all of her thoughts to the man she truly loved. If that meant accepting this young girl, she was a big enough person to do that.

What eventually smoothed any transition occurred the first evening Parker and Franny came over for dinner. Gabby and Franny hit it off immediately, solidified later when Franny was entered into the same school and was assigned to Gabby's homeroom class.

Myrna noted the far-off look in Parker's sad eyes. She sensed his pain and her loving heart ached along with his. Such was a significant bond. Parker realized once again what a wonderful person Myrna was. She made no demands and her mannerism was caring and intuitive. Myrna was a very special woman. While a love for Rhona would always lurk in the backdrop of his being, the affection he felt towards this woman was quite strong and would probably deepen further over time.

They married in a simple civil ceremony in June when classes were finished. A ready-made family of two daughters who were ecstatic at the turn of events rounded out the bliss. They settled in all together in Myrna's rented house, eagerly anticipating finding a home they might buy near the campus with a view of the mountains. Their future life together was affixed to their satisfying jobs at the University.

It was on a clear summer's night that Parker was restless in bed. He let up on his embrace of Myrna, kissed her gently on the cheek and went for a walk.

Because of this amazing woman his outlook had gained a clear focus. She was so forgiving, accepting and loving that he had made an astounding discovery. Just as the students who came to see him because they were floundering, being unsure and directionless can hover in many dimensions. Just as he had been in limbo during his younger years because he did not know what he wanted from life and the future was unclear, even after settling into a satisfying career he was still basically incomplete. It all made clear sense as brought to the surface by the significant impact of events. Through Myrna as an amazingly caring and affectionate woman he had discovered the fulfillment of love. Rhona had led the way, teaching him to open his eyes and his heart. The path to happiness can have many turns, many seemingly dead ends. There is no disgrace to have others take your hand and show you that the pathway continues beyond the thick foliage.

He did not realize that there was more for him to gain until the significance was totally absorbed in his being. Two daughters rounded out the scenario wonderfully. Surely this would make him a better person and a more understanding psychologist. He would also strive to be a good husband and father.

He returned to the house and the bed. Myrna stirred as he held her close. "Is there anything wrong?" she whispered in a sleep-laden voice.

"I love you. Nothing is wrong. Nothing could be better."

Live your questions now, and perhaps even without knowing it, you will live along some distant day into your answers.

Rainer Maria Rilke